WAITING FOR
ODYSSEUS

WAITING FOR ODYSSEUS

∾

A Novel

By
Clemence McLaren

Simon Pulse
New York London Toronto Sydney

ACKNOWLEDGMENTS

I want to thank my editor, Marcia Marshall,
who always pushes me to go deeper.

First Simon Pulse edition March 2004

Copyright © 2000 by Clemence McLaren

SIMON PULSE
An imprint of Simon & Schuster Children's Publishing Division
1230 Avenue of the Americas
New York, NY 10020

Also available in an Atheneum Books for Young Readers hardcover edition.
Designed by Michael Nelson
The text of this book was set in Bauer Bodoni.

Printed in the United States of America.
2 4 6 8 10 9 7 5 3 1

The Library of Congress has cataloged the hardcover edition as follows:
Waiting for Odysseus: a novel / by Clemence McLaren.—1st ed.
        p.   cm.
Summary: Presents the story of Odysseus's epic journey through the eyes of his faithful wife, Penelope, the sorceress Circe, the goddess Athena, and his old nanny Eurycleia.
ISBN 0-689-82875-6
1. Odysseus (Greek mythology)—Juvenile fiction. 2. Penelope (Greek mythology)—Juvenile fiction. 3. Circe (Greek mythology)—Juvenile fiction. 4. Athena (Greek deity)—Juvenile fiction. 5. Eurycleia (Greek mythology)—Juvenile fiction. [1. Odysseus (Greek mythology)—Fiction. 2. Penelope (Greek mythology)—Fiction. 3. Circe (Greek mythology)—Fiction. 4. Athena (Greek mythology)—Fiction. 5. Eurycleia (Greek mythology)—Fiction.]
I. Homer. Odyssey. II. Title PZ7.M78697Wai   2000   [Fic]—dc21
99-24572
ISBN 0-689-86705-0 (pbk.)

To my husband, Rob, my partner on this journey

∾

CONTENTS

WAITING FOR
ODYSSEUS

PART I

PENELOPE'S STORY:
A GIRL PLOTS A MARRIAGE

CHAPTER 1

∾

I loved him in that first moment. The Greeks believe love can strike like that, like sweet poison from an invisible arrow rushing through your veins. My hands shook, my legs went numb. I stumbled to the nearest wall and rested the wine jug I was carrying. Holding my breath, I watched him stride across the courtyard in his plain, unbleached tunic, confident as if he were wearing golden armor wrought by the gods. King of a small, barren island, he had no gold armor, no grand palace, no legitimate claim to such brazen confidence. His name was Odysseus.

"Look at him," our servant Hessia said. "Not a chance in the world, and he's parading in here like a prize stallion. . . ."

Odysseus had come to Sparta to court my cousin Helen, joining a dozen other suitors who were fast drinking up our reserves of wine. According to servant gossip, Helen had been fathered by the great god Zeus, and she was destined to be the most beautiful woman the world would ever know. All of the Greek kings wanted her. All of us paled in comparison to her spun-gold beauty. But this was the first time I'd ever felt jealous.

"Odysseus has as good a chance as any man here," I snapped, and Hessia looked at me suspiciously. "Here, take this wine and see that it's mixed properly," I said, eager to rid myself of her nosy presence. "And make sure Helen does her stint at the loom and doesn't go running off to the stable."

Both of us were charged with watching over my beautiful cousin. Hessia had been Helen's nursemaid, and when Helen's mother died, I'd been imported from my own home to serve as a civilizing influence. I was reserved and sensible and, even then at age twelve, already well trained in running a household and making fine cloth at the loom. My uncle, King Tyndareus, hoped his daughter would want to emulate me.

But to no avail. Four years later, I was sixteen, and Helen, a year younger, was still a wild spirit. On that particular day, her attention darted between the dowry clothes just arrived from Athens, the new foal in the stable, and the litter of kittens behind the stairs. She had no use for directing servants or taking inventory of food stocks, and little interest in her glorious destiny.

My own destiny was to be cast as the "true-hearted Penelope," but my celebrated virtue has been exaggerated. Love taught me to be devious. Right there in the courtyard, under the noon sun, I began plotting to have Odysseus for my husband—and all my life I have plotted to keep him.

Against all logic, I stood there on that first day trying to find a way to prevent him from meeting Helen. In truth, my splendid cousin took little notice of the kings vying for her hand, except to make fun of them. Most pitiful of all was stocky, red-haired Menelaus. He was brother to Agamemnon, high king over all Greece, who was already married to Helen's older sister. Poor Menelaus went speechless and beet red, redder than his hair, whenever Helen drifted by. Then there was huge, hulking Ajax—the largest man any of us had ever seen. We called him "Monster," but I knew Helen was secretly terrified of him.

Fortunately for me on that first afternoon, my cousin was scheduled to try on the new dowry clothes, and I stayed to supervise servants in the great hall. I was able to watch Odysseus from behind the columns of the adjoining vestibule. I sent a slave with a basin of scented water to wash his feet. I made sure he was supplied with the choicest cuts of meat and a basket of bread warm from the oven. The other suitors gathered for news of places he'd visited en route to Sparta. After a while, one of them asked him to entertain them.

Ajax called for silence. "Now that he's feasted, Odysseus can tell us one of his stories. He tells a better yarn than any of the bards. But don't be tempted to believe him. This man can charm the fish out of the ocean, and he has no reverence for the truth."

"That's because truth always depends on where the storyteller is standing," Odysseus replied, "and on what he wants. For are we not defined by our desires?" He beckoned for the steward. I had directed the man to pour our best ten-year-old Pramnian wine for Odysseus alone. I didn't think he'd noticed until he glanced over at me and raised his cup. A pulse throbbed in my temples. I looked away.

Then he began a story in his deep, melodious voice, the words pouring out like liquid. Ajax was right. Odysseus was more skilled than any bard. Lord of an insignificant island, with a farmer's homespun tunic, shoulders too broad for his height, and a thatch of sandy brown hair, he was really no match for the assembled kings. But his speech transformed him into a hero, and I understood why the men were so drawn to him.

It was inevitable that Helen would find me, that there would be some argument over the new clothes that would require my intervention.

"Penelope, Hessia says the turquoise robe is too short!" Helen said, tugging at my arm to get my attention. "She says I'm a disgrace. Look! Am I?"

Helen was radiant in the turquoise robe, the color mirroring the blue-green of her eyes.

"And you promised to braid my hair, with cornflowers entwined . . . remember? What are you waiting for?"

"Odysseus is telling a story about a king whose wife fell in love with a prize bull. . . ."

She looked over at him then. "Hessia says his island, Ithaca, has no running room for horses. No pastures of any kind. It's steep and rocky, only good for goats." She laughed, displaying perfect white teeth. "King of the Rocks!"

"He has more brains than all the others combined," I said, and then added, in a whisper, "Hush, he'll hear us."

It was too late. Odysseus had paused in his telling. The men turned in their chairs, devouring Helen with their eyes. I saw Odysseus taking full measure of her beauty, and I reached to pull at her veil so it would cover her lustrous gold hair. Suddenly, I wanted her dead, my sweet companion, dearer than any sister. Frightened by my murderous thoughts, I pushed her ahead of me out of the vestibule.

The next day Odysseus found me in the colonnade, which runs the length of the great hall.

"Lady Penelope. Thank you for the wine, for all your attentions. Are you always so gracious to visitors?"

"We try to observe the laws of hospitality." I lowered my eyes. It wasn't proper for an unmarried girl to be seen conversing with a man. And I was almost too breathless for speech. He'd taken the time to find out who I was! He'd spoken my name in his liquid bard's voice.

"Careful," he said with a teasing smile. "The others will lodge a complaint about special treatment."

"They're all too besotted to notice," I heard myself saying. I nodded at Helen across the courtyard.

"Ah, yes, the fabulous Helen."

But he had turned his gaze back to me. His eyes were brown, flecked with gold. "I can see she's completely dependent on you," he said. "What will happen when she goes off with one of these kings? Will you have to go along?"

"I never thought beyond her marriage," I lied. "I suppose my uncle will arrange something for me. Right now his overriding problem is what to do about them."

In the adjacent hall, Ajax and a lean, sharp-eyed king named Palamedes were yelling out bets in a game of draughts, played by tossing stones on a small table. Menelaus was throwing his spear at a target painted on the wall, to hoots of praise from the lesser kings.

Odysseus pointed with his chin. "Tyndareus is no

fool. He'll select the most powerful, and that's Menelaus. His brother Agamemnon receives tribute from all the Greek kings."

"No matter which one he chooses, it will likely provoke a war, the losers united against the winner and against Sparta. Meanwhile, the banquets are draining our treasury. No one knows how it will end." I smiled, shaking my head. "I won't bore you with the latest grain inventory."

"In that case, I'm even more grateful for the rare and delicious Pramnian wine."

Helen had spotted us. I stammered an excuse and ran to intercept her before she could come and stand next to me, outshining my darker hair and skin with her gold braids and ivory complexion.

After that, I forced myself to stay out of the great hall, afraid to be caught watching him. Still, I had a sixth sense for his movements, scanning for him at the edge of my vision whenever I passed along the colonnade. I took careful note of his habits. In the hall he often sat observing the action and thinking his thoughts, and once he almost seemed to be looking my way. In the twilight hour he liked to leave the city walls and walk in the olive grove.

On the third day, as the afternoon sun waned, I plaited my dark brown hair in a crown of braids entwined with fragrant flowers that I had taken all morning to select. I rubbed alkanet juice on my cheeks and put on my best white robe, cinching the waist with a silver belt that had arrived with Helen's dowry clothes. I reminded Helen that she needed to stay at the loom and practice the pattern I'd been teaching her.

"My border isn't going to look anything like yours," she complained, laughing, and then, "Penelope, you look lovely! What are you dressed up for?"

I shrugged. "I suppose I'm inspired by all the new clothes. Does the belt look all right?"

"You look beautiful! Here, let me tuck in this stem." She reached to adjust a gardenia woven into my braid. "Where are you going?"

"Out . . . to the orchard."

She narrowed her gaze.

"To gather some of the herbs for fever. From underneath the olive trees."

"You're wearing festival clothes to go pick herbs?"

Blushing furiously, I picked up my basket and ran off before she could ask any more questions.

"Wait," she called after me. "You forgot your veil!"

CHAPTER 2

I pretended to be surprised when I found Odysseus at the end of a row of trees, silhouetted against a rose-streaked sky. He came to meet me, taking my basket as he walked along beside me.

"The orchard reminds me of my farm back in Ithaca," he said, "and after a day with carousing suitors, I'm hungry for silence. Still, it's amusing to watch them casting glowering looks along with their javelins, flexing their muscles whenever Helen passes by. . . ."

"You don't seem distressed by your own poor prospects." I swallowed down a lump in my throat and went on. "Forgive me, My Lord, but you said yourself that Tyndareus is bound to select the wealthiest and most powerful of the kings."

"I have no expectations for myself. I'm only here to observe." He slowed his pace and glanced at me, his expression speculative. "And I don't begrudge Menelaus his prize. Helen's even more empty-headed than I expected her to be."

Automatically I jumped to her defense. "Really, she's not! She just . . . lives to enjoy the moment. Like a child. Like one of the immortals. She's not attached to the future. Never worries, never plans." I sighed. "Sometimes I wish I could be more like her."

He was studying me thoughtfully. "Your loyalty to your cousin makes you all the more admirable," he said softly.

I was caught in his mountain cat eyes, my heart thumping so loudly, I was certain he could hear it.

"For years I've tried to envision the wife I wanted to share my bed. Be mother to my children. . . ." He shook his head. "In an abstract way I could list qualities—beauty, intelligence, integrity. But she was always a hazy portrait in my mind's eye. . . ." I watched him take a deep breath and let it out.

"Until I met you," he said. "Until I saw your face, your quiet strength . . . You have a way of putting people at ease. Curse it, I'm not doing this well." His smile was surprisingly shy.

I didn't know how to respond. There were no rules for this conversation; such matters were always negotiated by a girl's father.

"I'm trying to tell you that Helen pales in comparison to her cousin Penelope. . . ."

And still I could find no voice. My soul was

standing aside, watching us walk side by side as the sky deepened from rose to violet. The world was hushed, holding its breath, and I understood that this was the most perfect moment I would ever know.

"If only I had something to bargain for your hand," he rushed on, as if reassured by my silence. "Your uncle no doubt intends you for the second-best king."

I inhaled the scent of wild oregano, an herb the Greeks call "joy of the mountains." I wanted to capture every detail, so I would remember always.

"*Zeus Thunderer, woman!* End my agony!" He dropped the basket and caught my arm. "Do you want me or not?"

I lifted my hand to his cheek. His skin was smooth and cool, his beard gold at the ends and brown underneath. "More than my life," I said, "from the moment you came striding across our court—looking like you owned the place."

Eyes shining, he unraveled my braid and combed out my hair with his fingers. He buried his face in it. "So fine and silky, just as I imagined it would be, and smelling like flowers."

I took a crushed gardenia, fallen from my braid, and held it up to him, my hand trembling. I kept wondering what Helen would say if she could see us—or my uncle Tyndareus. I twisted away to look over my shoulder.

"Don't be afraid; no one ever comes here at this

hour." He captured my face in his hands. "Penelope, my dearest love, I can't believe my good fortune, that you would give yourself to me. . . ."

I couldn't believe I was here in the orchard, without escort, without permission. That Odysseus wanted me, not Helen! All at once I felt proud, defiant, not at all like myself.

"I'm not afraid," I whispered.

In that slow pull toward one another, there was no more talk. I did not once think about my uncle's consent, though that was a significant obstacle to our marriage. The poets make much of this joining together of a man and a woman, but the sweetness of his touch, the mystery of his body, these were more magical than words can tell.

When I returned to the women's quarters, I looked at myself in the mirror, expecting to see some fundamental change. My cheeks were flushed, my eyes shining, as if with fever. I felt my life had only just begun, that everything else had been preparation for this day. I opened the shutters and stood gazing at the western horizon until the faint pink glow melted into blue. "How is it possible to be so happy?" I asked the gods.

But in the morning I began to search for a way to earn my uncle's blessing, to convince him to give me to the lord of a poor and backward island.

"Penelope, what's the matter with you?" Helen asked me several days later. She was at the mirror twisting ringlets into her bangs with a heated curling iron. "You've been standing at the loom for the longest time, just staring at the threads." When I didn't answer, she said, "Hessia saw you with him, coming up from the orchard; all the servants are gossiping."

I picked up my shuttle and thrust it in and out of the row of warp threads.

"Yesterday you were laughing together in the vestibule, where everyone could see." She smiled, watching my reaction. "He scares me with his brooding and his clever speeches. Whatever do you talk about?"

"The problem of your suitors, for one thing. Odysseus thinks he's found a way to select one of them without causing a war."

"But I don't *want* one of them. You *know* that!" She set down the curling iron and came over to the loom. "I want us to go on the way we've always been."

There was such pain in her blue-green eyes that I gathered her into my arms, still searching for words to tell her what had happened to me.

"Let's run away to the mountains, just the two of us," she said. "We can live on berries and nuts and not marry anyone."

"Dearest Helen, we've talked about this before. We'd starve to death in the mountains. We'd be captured by bandits and held for ransom. And there's no money to pay a ransom. Your suitors have drained the treasury." I stroked her flaxen hair. "It has to end. You see that, don't you?"

She shook her head, tears staining her pale cheeks. How I pitied her, pitied everyone who didn't know the miracle of love.

I never found the courage to tell her about Odysseus's famous solution. Helen had to hear of it from Hessia.

"Zeus All-Knowing, he's found a way to prevent bloodshed," the old nurse sputtered, red-faced and breathless from running to find us. "Come, hurry! Your father's about to announce it from the gallery. . . ."

"Wait, what's happening?" Helen asked as she ran along beside me. Hessia didn't stop to answer. For me, it was too late to try to explain. We arrived in the men's hall in time to watch the tall, white-haired king climb the stairs to the gallery and look down at the faces below.

"I have news you're all eager to hear," he yelled above the booming voices. The suitors noticed Helen's presence and gradually became silent, as if each man were dreaming of lying beside her in bed.

"Whoever wants to be considered for my daughter's hand will have to swear a sacred oath," Tyndareus said into the sudden hush.

"Me first!" Palamedes yelled; Ajax banged his great spear on the floor for silence.

"Hear me out, everyone!" the king went on.

"Before I announce my decision, you'll all have to swear an oath to Helen's husband: that you'll defend the man from anyone who envies his good fortune and tries to steal her away."

Their shouts subsided.

"For the rest of your lives! Like a blood brother . . ."

The suitors scanned one another's faces as the implications of this promise dawned on them. If they swore the oath and weren't chosen, they were prevented from ever attacking Helen's husband. Worse, they were honor bound to protect the man!

The king smiled down on them, knowing there would be no warfare among the suitors.

Later they sacrificed a horse at the altar underneath the gallery. It went to its death without a struggle, a good omen, showing the plan favorable to the gods, especially to Father Zeus, the All-Powerful. The priests cut the carcass into twelve sections. Each suitor stood next to one of them and repeated the oath.

"There were only twelve," Helen said when we were back in the women's quarters. "What happened to Odysseus? He wasn't there."

Hessia passed a hand over her forehead, frowning at me. "You were supposed to tell her," she said, and then, gently, to Helen, "He's been awarded Penelope . . . in exchange for his solution. Don't cry, my love. It's what we needed to get you married off."

"I don't want to be married off!"

Hessia took a short breath. "Penelope doesn't belong to you anymore. She's given her heart to him. You'll feel that way about your husband when the time comes."

"No, I won't!" Helen cried. "Not ever!" Twisting away, she lashed out at my loom and sent it crashing to the floor.

"This was *your* doing!" she yelled from the doorway. "The oath, everything! *You* gave him the idea. I'll never forgive you."

Helen did forgive me after all, four years into her marriage to Menelaus, when she herself felt the sweet sting of love's arrow. But it wasn't Menelaus she fell in love with. It was a beautiful Trojan prince who launched a great war by carrying her away. And in the end I was the one who never forgave her.

CHAPTER 3

∾

I loved everything about Ithaca, the quiet island rhythms, the rocky hillsides dotted with sheep and wildflowers, and especially the palace, which was really just a well-built country manor, open to mountain views and salty breezes.

Odysseus feared I would miss the luxury of my mainland home. He brought in a master craftsman to make me a chair with a footrest, inlaid with whorls of silver and ivory. My husband built our bedroom himself, walling in a favorite courtyard. He carved our marriage bed out of a large olive tree that was still alive and rooted in the earth. Shutters closed, working by torchlight, he capped the trunk and made it into one of the bedposts.

"I want the olive tree to be our secret," he told me on the night our bed was finished.

"You know nothing escapes notice of Eurycleia,"

I said, smiling. Eurycleia had been my husband's
nurse when he was a baby. Odysseus's father had
bought her for the worth of twenty oxen just before
his son was born. Recognizing her intelligence and
loyalty, he eventually gave her the keys to the household. He also avoided sleeping with her, so as to have
no discord with his wife. In turn, Odysseus's mother
allowed Eurycleia unchallenged rule over servants
and slaves alike. Now, hair graying at the temples,
she stood ready to anticipate my husband's every
wish.

Odysseus said, "Oh, her, yes, but she'll keep it to
herself."

I was standing with one hand on the olive tree
bedpost, admiring the cream-colored blankets I had
woven and admiring my husband, who was stretched
out beneath them. I knelt beside him and kissed his
eyes. "You can count on my silence," I whispered.

"Everyone knows olive trees live forever," he
said, pulling me down beside him. "The spirits of the
tree are pulsing through us as we lie here. We're sure
to produce strong sons and beautiful daughters."

When Odysseus brought me from Sparta,
Eurycleia had stayed aloof. She went on running the
house as if I weren't there, which meant that the
serving women ignored me as well. I was careful not
to cross her. She had her own precise rituals for mixing wine, kneading bread, and carving meat, and she

wanted it all done with no dawdling. "Snap to it!" she'd yell at the poor maids. "My hair will turn white by the time those floors are swept!"

In only one thing did I defy her household routines—the care of the olive tree bed. I wove sheets of pure linen and insisted on drying them on a field of wild lavender that grew in a nearby valley. She'd sniff and mumble, "Stuff and nonsense," whenever she saw me carrying them back to the palace, carefully folded and giving off the sweet, crisp odor that mainland women know will promote good dreams.

Most brides have trouble with their mothers-in-law. Mine was sweet and passive. It was Eurycleia I used to curse when no one was looking. She worshiped Odysseus. I knew she'd never find a woman worthy of him. And even though I was hardworking and sensible, I could find no way to earn her approval—not until my pregnancy began to show. She'd surprise me then with a half smile, looking down at my pattern on the loom. Toward the end she served me wine the household was saving for festivals. And on the day I gave her a new, healthy manchild to fuss over, she at last decided to accept me into the family.

It was the end of my second year in Ithaca. Eurycleia had presided over the birth.

"Zeus Thunderer, give the love some breathing room," she said, pushing past Odysseus with a cup of honeyed wine. "Good girl, that's right, sip it down.

You did fine. No yelling and swearing, got the job done proper like."

I exchanged a secret look with my husband. For Eurycleia there was even a proper way to give birth, with no yelling and swearing. I smiled at the small bundle Odysseus was holding so reverently in the crook of his arm, this son who was the answer to all our prayers. It was a miracle that he was finally here, sharing our world. It was a miracle that the pain was over so much more suddenly than it began.

"Here, look alive," Eurycleia snapped at one of the slaves. "Get that other pillow and watch her head. Don't lift it like a sack of grain! Althira will massage you to make sure you've passed all the afterbirth," she said to me. "She has the best hands of any of the servants." And then, to Odysseus, she said, "What about a name? How shall we call this new master?"

"Telemachus," he said.

The name meant "final battle"; I felt a quiver of fear.

"Ah, the war with Troy," Eurycleia said. "Are you sure that's not a bad omen?"

My husband didn't answer. His expression unreadable, he stood looking down at the tiny, sleeping face.

Rumors of a war with Troy, our wealthy neighbors across the Aegean Sea, had been drifting to the islands from the Greek mainland for more than a year. I can't isolate the moment when they began to dominate talk in the servants' quarters, the moment when our perfect world began to shift on its axis. But it was sometime later. On the night of our son's birth, I was too joyful to worry about the future.

I should have known those years were too precious to last. But, even if I had known, I could not have savored them any more. Oracles had long predicted this great war, and there were compelling political reasons for it. Located at the entrance to the Black Sea, Troy collected taxes on all commerce that sailed in and out. The Greek kings depended on imported corn from Asia, but they knew better than to start a war over the customs duties charged by the Trojan king, a man named Priam, who was well favored by the gods. Father Zeus was said to love Troy above all other nations.

And then, in the third year of our marriage, my cousin Helen gave the Greeks the excuse they needed. It was the season of the wine harvest, just before my son's first birthday, when Helen ran away with one of Priam's fifty sons, a Trojan prince called Paris Alexandros. Helen's husband, Menelaus, had apparently opened negotiations with Troy over trade tariffs, and Paris had come to Sparta as his kingdom's official representative. There he met Helen, who, from then on, would forever be known as Helen of Troy.

By the time my child was weaned from my breast, Helen and Paris had fled to the safety of Troy's lofty walls, leaving the world in an uproar and Menelaus preparing for battle. I can imagine my sweet childhood companion falling victim to the invisible arrows sent by Aphrodite, goddess of love. Still, I have never been able to forgive my cousin for launching the fleet of Greek ships toward Troy, a word I can hardly bear to speak even now.

Of course the kings who'd sworn the Oath of the Horse were all eager to earn Greek glory and Trojan gold. They called the event a kidnapping. Most everyone else, Odysseus included, thought otherwise and made jokes about poor Menelaus, the jilted husband. "After all," Odysseus said, laughing, "Paris had only a small contingent of men. He could not have removed Helen and her treasure without her consent."

"They cannot make you go to war," I interrupted. "You never swore the oath to defend her husband."

"How can I reassure you, my love? I have no wish to join this campaign."

I glanced over at Telemachus, who was tossing stones for the game of draughts, his small hand guided by Eurycleia.

I said, "They won't let you stay behind. They need you too much."

"What can the Greek kings do, tie me up and

throw me onboard one of their red ships? Besides, you exaggerate my reputation as a warrior. Come, cheer up, you're losing all perspective over these rumors."

I forced a smile, always so eager to please him. But I knew they would not have to tie him up. They would only need to appeal to his honor.

CHAPTER 4

∾

Phoenician traders reported seeing the Greek fleet assembling at the Bay of Aulis, commanded by High King Agamemnon, older brother to Menelaus. An old seer who read the flights of birds prophesied that my husband would sail with them and would not return for nineteen years.

We never talked about this prediction, though it was common gossip in the town. Still, I knew they would come for him, even as I struggled to find a way to keep him home. Rising before dawn to scan the bay for Greek ships, I was first to spot Palamedes' galley—the red speck on the horizon that would cancel my happiness.

I found Odysseus lacing up his leather vest to go welcome whatever visitors were sailing into port.

"I know of a way to trick them!" I cried out.

He looked at me with pity in his eyes. "Dearest

Penelope, they cannot compel me to go. You've said so yourself. I never swore the oath."

"Hear my plan . . . for our son's sake." I knelt at his feet, sobbing quietly. "They will not be put off so easily. They have to think you're incapable of serving their cause."

He lifted me to my feet and wrapped his arms around me. "All right, tell me your plan."

Odysseus didn't go down to the harbor to welcome the ship. When Palamedes arrived, my husband was working in the fields wearing filthy clothes and a pointed foolscap. Instead of oxen, he'd hitched two goats to his plow, and he was weaving in and out of furrows, pretending not to see his royal guests. Palamedes and an older king named Nestor stopped to watch underneath a stand of trees.

Having captured their attention, Odysseus laughed a cackling laugh as he grabbed a handful of salt from his pouch and cast it onto the earth.

"He's been like this for weeks," I told Palamedes, approaching with Telemachus on my hip. I'd brought along the child to enlist their pity, an idea that turned out to be a fatal mistake. I said, "He's been sowing his fields with salt instead of seeds. When he's not out here, he's sitting on the dung heap ranting and tearing his hair."

Palamedes narrowed his ferret eyes, squinting into the morning sun.

"My Lord, I apologize for this poor hospitality. . . ."

Only desperation could have made me think I could fool Palamedes, who had a reputation for cunning that was almost equal to my husband's. It happened with no warning. His glance darted from me to Odysseus. Suddenly, he leaped forward and snatched my son from my arms. He ran into the field and, stooping, placed the child directly in the path of my husband's plow.

"Let's see if you're crazy enough to run over your son!" Palamedes shouted.

Of course Odysseus pulled to a stop and knelt to pick up Telemachus, who was only then beginning to cry.

"Stop this nonsense, Odysseus," Palamedes said. "Obviously you're sane enough to go to war."

Telemachus's wails pierced the silence.

"Indeed, a certain madness is a requirement for war," Odysseus said, looking down at his son, stroking the boy's silky hair.

"Odysseus, raider of cities, you know you're itching to feel the heft of a good sword in your hand." Palamedes smiled his crooked smile. "Admit it."

Odysseus dropped his eyes, and I knew this charge was at least partly true.

"Besides," Palamedes was saying, "wars are won by superior tactics and the gods' favor, both of which you possess in abundance. You cannot refuse your countrymen in this time of humiliation."

I stood there hugging my sides, hating them both.

Palamedes and Nestor spent the day telling Odysseus about the Greek coalition—the water and food supplies, the men and ships already arrived at Aulis, a bay on the coast opposite Troy. Agamemnon had sent the two kings to enlist Odysseus and a second warrior, whose presence was even more crucial to a Greek victory—a young man called Achilles, the son of a mortal king and a minor sea goddess. Oracles had prophesied that the Trojan War would not be won without him, but he had disappeared. According to the prophets, Achilles had a choice of destinies. He could lead either a long, uneventful life at home, or a short, glorious life fighting and dying in the Trojan War. Naturally, his mother, Thetis, was determined to secure the long, peaceful destiny for her only son.

"We think we know where she's hidden him," Palamedes said.

Nestor, who was famous for long-winded speeches, launched into the story. "She's put him with relatives on Scyros. Living in the women's quarters disguised as a girl! But there are rumors. . . ." Grinning, the gray-bearded warrior slapped his knee. "The young stud has got one of the cousins pregnant."

Palamedes leaned forward. "I don't think the boy

will offer much resistance, but we need Odysseus, master of disguises, to get close to him."

Like my husband's reputation as raider of cities, this was another side of him I had never seen. It made me wonder if I knew him at all.

Odysseus, Nestor, and Palamedes spent the better part of a month sailing to Scyros, where Odysseus had little trouble persuading Achilles to leave with them. My husband told the story in the men's hall the night they returned with the boy to Ithaca.

Arriving on Scyros, Odysseus had dressed as a peddler and visited the king's daughters with a pack full of shimmering veils, jewel-encrusted robes, and bronze mirrors from the Orient. The girls quivered with excitement, squealing and grabbing at his wares.

"All except one tall, ungainly maiden," my husband said slowly, drawing out the suspense. "She stood aside, arms crossed over her chest, smiling scornfully until I withdrew from its wrappings a magnificent sword, a gift to my father from Agamemnon. . . ."

The men in the hall sat forward in their chairs, charmed by my husband's liquid voice.

"Then this tall, muscular maiden sprang forward and grabbed the sword, swishing it around her head." Odysseus laughed, pointing at Achilles. "And here she—he—sits, ready to shed Trojan blood!"

That's how I came to know Achilles. The boy

who would soon strike terror into the hearts of Trojans was still a beardless youth unstained by the blood of battle, but even then there was something terrible about his thin-lipped smile. I knew he would relish the killing, that it would be, for him, like an act of love to plunge his sword into the body of an enemy warrior—or maybe a fellow Greek. I was afraid my husband—or even High King Agamemnon—would never be able to manage him.

The next day, Palamedes and Nestor sailed for Aulis to deliver their prize warrior to Agamemnon. Odysseus stayed behind for another month to gather his fleet of twelve vessels from Ithaca, the mainland, and neighboring islands. But I had already lost him. Just once, I wanted to walk together at sunset in the orchard, to imprint that moment into my husband's memory. He never found the time. On the rare nights he held me in our olive tree bed, he was still thinking about provisioning ships and recruiting foot soldiers from the villages.

The morning he left, I brought my parting gifts—a finely woven tunic, a fleecy maroon cape, and to clasp it, a brooch in the shape of his favorite hunting dog, Argos. I'd commissioned the piece from a master goldsmith to remind Odysseus of the good life he was leaving behind.

We had only moments alone. After packing my gifts, he sat down on the bed and reached for my hands, looking up at me. "Take care of my parents, as you have always done," he said. "I leave all things in your charge. Mentor will instruct our son in the martial arts. The old warrior will be a friend to you, too." I held his head against my breasts, drinking in the smell of his hair.

"But if I don't return . . ."

"Please . . . that cannot happen. I would die."

"Let us not lie to one another; we've never done that. Here, sit beside me so I can look at you." He stroked my face. "My beautiful Penelope, these years with you have given me more happiness than I could have known how to ask for." Then, after a silence, he said, "The Trojans are skilled warriors. Not every Greek will make it home."

I bit my lip, tasting blood on my tongue.

"When you see a beard on our son's face, you must marry again."

"Never!"

"Look at me, Penelope! When our son becomes a man, you must leave this house for Telemachus to rule. Make a new life for yourself."

I twisted away, covering my mouth with my hand. I felt sick to my stomach.

"You cannot wait for me forever. Promise me, Penelope!"

There was a knock on the door, and then Mentor's voice. "Master, the rations are loaded in the hull, all the wine jars, barley meal double wrapped in leather sacks. Shall I order the crews to man the oars?"

∽ ∽ ∽

Down at the port I watched Odysseus holding the mast of his blue-prowed ship, shouting orders as if he had no thought for me or our son. I watched the ships drift toward the horizon, water churning behind each rhythmic stroke of the oars. Seven hundred men in twelve ships, and not all of them would return. Selfishness gripped my heart as I stood there, making bargains with the gods. *I don't care about any of the others. Only Odysseus has to return. Please let him return.*

Eurycleia stayed beside me and held my arm. I was grateful she didn't try to cheer me with false hopefulness. My throat ached; I longed for the release of tears as the ships disappeared into the summer haze. But I was the queen. People were watching, expecting composure.

"I hate him for leaving us," I said between my teeth.

"For shame!" Eurycleia whispered. "That's not like you at all!"

"He told me he wouldn't go! He could have refused!"

"You cannot blame him for following his warrior's heart. And his destiny."

"What's to be *my* destiny?"

Eurycleia didn't answer. We both knew that my destiny was to wait, to become expert at waiting.

I need not tell of the great war; traveling bards sing of it all over the civilized world. Only one thing:

I was right about Achilles. He did not submit to his commander's authority. He and Agamemnon hated one another on sight, and conflict erupted into revolt when Agamemnon took a favorite slave girl Achilles had captured in a raid. Only my husband's intervention kept the boy from attacking his chief.

As nine years of siege outside Troy's walls dragged on, stories drifted to us of Odysseus's courage and ingenious tactics. It was said that the great Athena, goddess of war and wisdom, fought at his side, that the wooden horse that ended the siege was his design. In time, I created an image from these stories, and it became more real than the man I had known.

After the war, Odysseus and his men sailed for home, flushed with victory and loaded with Trojan gold. But a squall blew them off course to the Land of the Lotus-eaters, where friendly natives fed some of them a magical fruit, which erased all memory of home. Although badly in need of food, Odysseus drove his men to sail on. The next landfall belonged to the Cyclops, a savage race of one-eyed giants descended from the sea god, Poseidon. A search party located a cave well supplied with cheeses and sheep; the men wanted to help themselves and sail away. Of course, Odysseus was too honorable to take food without meeting the owner, asking for hospitality, and trading wine in exchange.

But there was no hospitality when the one-eyed

giant, whose name was Polyphemus, returned home. He trapped them inside with a huge boulder and promptly devoured six of the men, crunching their bones and wiping blood off his chin with the back of his hand while their shipmates watched in horror. Odysseus refused to give way to panic. He offered the giant bowl after bowl of undiluted wine. When Polyphemus passed out drunk, Odysseus had them sharpen a tree trunk, which they used like a battering ram to put out the Cyclops's only eye. They escaped the next morning when the blinded Polyphemus let his sheep out to pasture.

But this rescue would earn my husband the wrath of Poseidon, for Polyphemus was not only the sea god's descendant, he was the god's favorite son. And from that day forward, the blue-maned Poseidon, who rules the oceans that wrap the earth, was determined that Odysseus and his loyal shipmates would never reach home.

PART II

CIRCE'S STORY:
A WITCH TAKES A LOVER

CHAPTER 1

~

I once asked Odysseus, "How did Poseidon know it was you who blinded his son?"

"I told Polyphemus who I was!" he said. "We were making our escape from the Cyclops's island, my men all rowing for their lives. I stood on the prow and shouted out my name. 'Odysseus, son of Laertes, from the island of Ithaca! I'm the one who blinded you, you man-eating monster! Got my men out of your filthy cave, tied to the bellies of your sheep! Got your sheep, too!'"

"Your men must have begged you to stop baiting him," I said, interrupting.

"I suppose so. The giant was hurling boulders down at our ship, guided by my voice—" He stole a glance at my half smile and went on. "How could I be silent? It was a matter of honor."

I looked away and shrugged my shoulders. What

can you expect? Here was this man, driven by a male ego even more monumental than most. Because of it, his legendary cleverness couldn't save him from acts of devastating foolishness. And it was this foolishness that landed Odysseus on my island with only one ship left in his fleet.

I am Circe, the sorceress, and I had been waiting for him for a very long time. That is, I always knew he would come to my island after the fall of Troy. I didn't know the golden brown of his eyes or the sound of his voice. I didn't know what it would be like to love a man who was not afraid to resist.

His journey to me began well enough, as he later took pains to describe, his exploits growing more glorious with each retelling.

"In the Land of the Lotus-eaters," he told me, "the flowery fruit made my men forget they had a home to return to. I had to drag them back to the ships and lash them to the benches." He shook his head. "They wanted to stay there forever. Some were clinging to trees; other fools were running off into the bushes."

On the afternoon of this particular retelling, we were lying in a green meadow, our bodies amber in the late afternoon sun.

"In the Land of the Lotus-eaters," I observed, "you behaved sensibly because none of the natives threatened your pride. All they wanted was to share their sweet, addictive fruit with any visitors who

came their way." I traced the planes of his cheekbones with my fingertips. "Nobody was looking for a
contest with a great hero."

"How can you know what it means to be a hero?
Have some respect, woman."

"I'm not a woman, I'm a goddess."

"A witch," he said, planting kisses on my throat.

But I would not be distracted. "Heroic boasting,"
I said. "But to boast of your escape to Polyphemus,
favorite son of Poseidon? To give your name, your
father's name, your home island? Did that make
sense?" I picked a red poppy from the meadow grass
and tucked it behind his ear. "You've already told me
what happened after that."

"Right sorry I am that I did." He released me
and sat up.

"Ah, yes," I said, smiling. "The blinded Cyclops
threw back his head and bellowed to the great ocean,
'Hear me, Poseidon. If I am truly your son, grant that
Odysseus, from the island of Ithaca, may never
return home!' So now you've got the god of the
oceans out to destroy you—and you a sea captain!"

Odysseus laughed ruefully. "Circe, you promised
not to unman me, yet you torture me with words."

"You shouldn't have been in that cave in the first
place. Everyone knows the Cyclops have no respect
for the laws of hospitality. You should have taken
your food and run. Only a fool would have stayed to
meet the monster."

He snatched the poppy from his ear and crushed it in his hand. "I was curious. I wanted to see what sort of creature lived there."

"You wanted to see if you could match his strength."

"It's not just about fighting," he said, turning away.

I stopped teasing then, because I was in danger of spoiling our golden afternoon. I knelt behind him and wrapped my arms around his neck, my breasts against his broad back. "Let's not talk anymore," I whispered into his ear.

But Odysseus didn't give up so easily. Later that night he reopened the debate while we were lying in bed.

"All right, then," he said, "what about my meeting with Aeolos, king of the winds? You have to admit that was a triumph of pure diplomacy, not muscle. He was so impressed with my war stories that he gave me a present of all the winds captured inside a leather bag."

"I know. All except the West Wind, the one you needed to push you home to Ithaca. And again, you would have gotten home—except for your pride."

I felt him stiffen in the darkness. "What new faultfinding is this?"

"You wouldn't tell your men what was inside that bag. Wouldn't let them near it. Think about it. Have you ever been forbidden to look inside a bag?"

Odysseus understood where I was leading. "Enough," he said. "I will hear no more."

At that point in the discussion, Odysseus got up and stomped away. But let me finish the story of Aeolos's bag of winds. Odysseus's men decided it was full of treasure and that their captain wasn't going to share any of it. Why else, they thought, would he remain awake steering the ship for nine days straight? They were within sight of Ithaca when Odysseus fell into a deep sleep. (You will see that he tends to fall asleep at inconvenient moments.) The louts seized the bag and pulled the silver cord, releasing a fearful windstorm that tossed their ship back into the open seas. When Odysseus woke to see his home coast fading into the distance, he wanted to leap into the roiling waves and drown himself.

With Poseidon in charge, things got worse before they got better. The sea god delivered them to another race of savage giants, the Laestragonians. Always needing food and water, the fleet moored inside the narrow harbor, which soon became a death trap for all but one of the twelve ships. Only Odysseus escaped with his native Ithacans. Poseidon wasn't finished with him.

That's when the gods sent him to me. With shattered hearts his surviving crew landed on my silent shore. They saw smoke spiraling up from a wooded hilltop. Odysseus went to hunt for game while a search party followed the smoke to my marble palace, shining like a jewel in the green woods.

They should have been warned off by the mountain lions and wolves skulking outside, not at all vicious but wagging their tails and looking at them with their yellow eyes as if wanting desperately to speak.

But luring them into my trap was easy. It always is. They'd been months at sea with no women and no comforts of home. They pressed their faces to the window and saw me weaving a silver web at my loom. They heard me singing a love song. They smelled bread baking in my oven. They called for me to let them in.

I didn't know that one of them had remained outside, a suspicious chap named Eurylochus. From the window he watched me welcome the others with wine. He saw me serve barley and cheese, sweetened with honey to hide the taste of my magic potion. He saw me go around and touch each man with my wand.

"We've a need for more pigs," I said. As they gaped at one another in horror, their bodies grew coarse hairs, their ears grew pointed, and their noses flattened into snouts.

Wild-eyed and babbling, Eurylochus tore off down the hill. When he got to the ship, he was almost too distraught to tell his story. Of course, I knew nothing of the witness. I took my new livestock to the sty and threw acorns to them while they squealed miserably, shedding human tears from their piggy eyes. I always let them keep their men's minds inside their new bodies; this made them more interesting to watch.

Still, I was already bored with them. It had become routine, this business of changing men into animals. When I first arrived on the island after the death of my husband, it had been a way to pass the time, to get even with the human race. But it was no longer exciting, this power I had over victims coming from the sea.

Some time later another sailor appeared at the window. I could tell he was their leader by the way he came strutting in when I opened the door. I offered him wine in a golden cup and my barley mixture, which he ate with a smug smile.

I didn't know who he was. I didn't know a god was watching over him. I tapped him with my wand and said, "Come to the sty and you can wallow with your companions."

Nothing happened except that he pulled out his sword.

I felt fear in my stomach, then the thrill of recognition. "Odysseus!" I cried.

This disconcerted him; he lowered his sword.

"It was prophesied that you would come! Hermes, the messenger, has given you a moly flower, the antidote to my potion. Surely that's what must have happened, otherwise you would be joining your crew in the sty."

He raised his sword to my throat. "What have you done with my men?"

"Your men are safe," I said, keeping my voice calm and rational.

At last he set down the sword and pulled the moly flower from his tunic, its black root still attached. "It's true," he said. "Hermes met me on the path. He told me this was the palace of Circe, the sorceress. He said you would order me to your bed when you learned that your spell hadn't worked."

I laughed at his outraged expression. "You cannot refuse a sorceress; he must have told you that, too."

I hate to admit it, but Hermes' magic is superior to mine. He had not only made this man immune to my spells; he had endowed him with uncommon beauty. And it wasn't only Hermes watching over Odysseus. The goddess Athena, favorite daughter of the great Zeus, was said to love this man above all others. I was sure she'd sent Hermes on this afternoon's errand. She was always fussing over Odysseus. He was like the son this committed virgin was never going to have.

"Do you order all your visitors to your bed?" he demanded.

"No, hardly ever. I prefer changing shipwrecked sailors into pigs—animals that don't befoul the earth

with their endless battles. I have no desire to procre-
ate. I haven't wanted a man in my bed for some
time. . . ." I stopped to ask myself, *Why is this one so
alluring, then? Because he's protected by powerful
gods . . . and he could prove entertaining for a time.*

I took his hand. He did not protest. I led him to
my sleeping platform and pulled back shimmering
curtains to reveal fine coverlets and bedposts inlaid
with ivory and gold. The scent of honeysuckle hung
in the air like motes drifting in light. He stood looking down at the bed for the longest time. He must
have been remembering the clean, sweet smell of
sheets, the softness of his wife's skin. I remember
thinking, *So there's more to this man, this raider of
cities.*

Odysseus was the only Greek king who took no
concubine, who wanted none of the Trojan princesses
for his prize. What was it that kept this lusty warrior
from taking comfort in the arms of a woman?
Intrigued, I pulled the clip from my braid and let my
pale hair flow down over my shoulders. I moved my
hands up his chest and laced them behind his neck,
pressing against him, my body warm and soft under
my silk robe.

He groaned softly. His lips grazed my cheek,
then, pulling away, he said, "How can I trust you
when you've turned my men into pigs? I refuse to
enter your bed until you swear an oath that you
won't unman me when I'm lying naked beside you."

"Such insolence, and from a mere mortal."

"Swear that you won't take away my power."

Let me tell you something about men. They're more afraid of being unmanned than of being transformed into pigs. Still, I found his resistance interesting. More than interesting. This man was refusing to enter my bed, and it was more exhilarating than anything that had happened since I'd come to this island.

I swore a sacred oath to do him no harm. He nodded gravely. Eyes shut, he traced my lips as if his fingers were remembering the feel of a woman.

"How long has it been?" I asked.

"So beautiful," he whispered.

I breathed his smell into my body, like crushed ferns. I tasted the sea salt on his muscled shoulders. Then I closed the curtains behind us, and, bathed in shifting sunlight, we enjoyed the gift of love.

After we came out from the sleeping platform, my maids took Odysseus to a bathing pool, where they sponged warm water over his head and shoulders. He submitted without a word as they rubbed him with rose oil and dressed him in a tunic I'd woven myself. Meanwhile, stewards were mixing wine in a silver bowl. Serving women brought bread and fruit in gold baskets, while carvers sliced off the choicest cuts of meat. But when I led Odysseus to an armchair and placed a footstool under his feet, he sat staring at the banquet spread before him.

"You needn't be afraid to eat and drink," I said, thrusting a goblet at him. "I've already sworn an oath not to harm you."

"How could I enjoy this feast?"—his lips tightened—"My men are in your pigsty! If you really want to be kind to me, you'll release them from your spell."

"Mortals! I'll never understand your irrational attachments. They must be a constant source of pain." I grabbed his hand. "Come!"

My wand held high, I led him through spacious halls and out to the sty. When I flung open the gate, the pigs rushed to Odysseus, squealing their sad, unintelligible stories. One by one, I tapped them with the wand. Their bristles fell away, their snouts shrunk back into noses. They became the men they once were, only better. To demonstrate my goodwill, I'd made them taller and handsomer, as youthful as when they'd left home.

Wouldn't you think they'd thank me for this deliverance? But, no, they grabbed Odysseus's hands, sobbing in gratitude. Still, I was touched by their tearful reunion—I had never before released a man from the spell—so touched that I told Odysseus to go fetch the rest of his men from the ship.

The seaman Eurylochus, who was witness to my magic, tried to prevent his colleagues from going up to the palace. Made bold by terror, he shouted at Odysseus, "She's a witch, and she's cast her spell on *you*, too!" And then, to the men, he said, "Remember the Cyclops's cave? Six of us killed because our captain wouldn't listen to us. You'll all be turned into pigs if you follow him now!"

Odysseus wanted to lop off his head for insubordination; the men held him back. "Let him stay and guard the ship," one suggested. In the end they all followed behind Odysseus, and Eurylochus was too afraid to stay behind. They found their comrades feasting merrily and rushed to embrace them, whooping and laughing. The men who'd been pigs had been bathed and massaged with precious oils, and each one was attended by a beautiful and compliant nymph.

Odysseus stood aside and watched, perhaps remembering such feasts before the war. Remembering his wife.

What must it be like, I wondered, to be joined to the same partner all your mortal days? To eat and drink, share secret jokes, to fight and make love afterward. To wake up beside this person and feel happy.

My own marriage—to the king of the Sarmatians—had been a series of conflicts with no lovemaking afterward. My husband, for all his bluster, was secretly terrified of my magic. Still, it's not true what they say. He died of food poisoning, some bad fish. But people will believe what they believe. They say the gods exiled me to this island.

I exiled myself. Now I live in a splendid palace surrounded by servants and fawning animals. They are all afraid of me.

As I watched Odysseus, I found myself envying a mere mortal.

I should have sent him back to his ship and conjured favorable winds to speed him home to Ithaca. Instead, I went and took his face in my hands. "No more grieving, my greathearted Odysseus," I said. "You have suffered much. Here you will eat and drink just as you did back in Ithaca. You will sleep in a clean bed. You will forget all your wanderings, and I will fill your ears with music."

CHAPTER 2

❧

One year passed in a dream, but Odysseus did not forget. He held Ithaca always in his heart. Lying beside me in bed, he dreamed of his Penelope. She was woven into all his dreams of home. One night I awoke to find him at the window, gazing down at a moonlit sea.

He saw me and came to kneel at my feet. "Circe, keep the promise you made"—he shot a quick look up at me—"that you would help me get home."

"I made no such promise, my much conniving Odysseus. Save your schemes for your fellow mortals, whose memories are imperfect at best."

Anger flashed in his eyes, but he instantly controlled himself. "Please," he said.

I quelled the fear that rose in my chest. What was the matter with me? I always knew this moment would come. "I will help you, of course," I said slowly. "I would never keep a man against his will."

He kissed my palm. "My beautiful benefactress."

"Don't be too quick to thank me. Before you sail for home, the oracles insist you must undertake another journey, a journey more terrible than anything you've known so far."

"What could be more terrible than the daily slaughter at Troy? Or watching the Cyclops chew up my men and spit out their bones?"

"I will tell you, my love." I was silent a moment. "It will perhaps convince you to stay here with me."

The place humans fear above all others is Hades, the shadowy land where they all must go after they die. It lies at the end of the earth, beyond the great oceans. When I told Odysseus he would have to travel there, he was speechless with terror, the only time I'd ever seen him at a loss for words.

I said, "According to the oracles, you will never reach home if you don't first find the prophet, Teresias, whose wisdom remains intact, even in death. He has secret instructions for you . . . and news of your Penelope."

"No one has visited Hades and lived to return. How would I sail there? Who would guide me?"

So he was not deterred. I took a long, steadying breath. "The North Wind will push you through ocean streams and into the dark river that separates the Land of the Living from the Land of the Dead.

When you arrive, you must perform sacrifices exactly as I tell you."

I spent the rest of the night explaining the secret rituals he needed to perform in order to gain an audience with Teresias and then be allowed to return to the Land of the Living.

At dawn he roused his men, and they loaded the ship, their faces grim. Wisely, Odysseus had told them what danger they were sailing into. They rowed into the waiting current; at once the North Wind filled their sails and swept them out to sea.

I'd been tempted to keep him with me. I had the power. But standing there at the water's edge, I understood that there had always been a great loneliness linked to my power, a loneliness that would pool even deeper if I forced him to stay. This I knew for certain; all the rest was confusion.

One crewman was not onboard Odysseus's ship. After a night of drinking and carousing, a dull-witted lad named Elpenor had climbed up on my roof to enjoy the full moon. Roused by the commotion at daybreak, the fool staggered to the ladder and fell off, breaking his neck. I found his body as soon as I returned to the palace.

Poor Elpenor was the first ghost Odysseus met in Hades; his spirit had traveled faster than their ship. Before Odysseus went off in search of Teresias, he had to promise Elpenor that when the mission in Hades was complete, he would return to my island to collect his body and perform the proper funeral rites. For reasons I've never understood, mortals set great importance on what happens to their bodily shells after the spirit has departed.

So I had to face a second good-bye. After their release from Hades, Odysseus and his men returned to claim their crewman's body, which they burned, according to their custom, along with his armor. I waited in my palace until the men had made their farewells and shed their tears, then I put on a glistening silver robe, tied a jeweled belt around my waist, and went down to the harbor. My servants followed with food and wine.

"Come and eat," I told the men. "Let my nymphs entertain you, for tomorrow at dawn you'll have a new journey to test your courage."

I took Odysseus's hand and led him away from the camp to a favorite cove. His manner was distracted; already his heart and mind were elsewhere. Lying beside me under the stars, he talked of his meeting with Teresias, who'd given him news of events in Ithaca.

"Presumptuous men are occupying my hall, eating up my resources. Men whose families I protected when I was their king. . . ." He bolted upright, hugging his knees. "They're courting my wife, refusing to leave until she chooses one of them!"

Penelope again! I savored an image of Odysseus returning home to find her locked in the arms of a youthful suitor. I said, "She must find the attention quite stimulating . . . after all these years."

He wasn't listening. "No one can control them," he was saying. "My father's retreated to his farm, living like a hermit. My mother died of her grief! I talked to her ghost, there in Hades. . . ." He dropped his face into his hands. "I kept reaching for her, trying to hold her in my arms, but I couldn't. Their bodies have no substance. . . . *Dead, because of her love for me!*"

"Mortals really die from love?"

"It's not so difficult. She stopped wanting to be alive. Stopped eating. How thin and pale she was. It broke my heart to look at her."

"Such vulnerability. It's a wonder women keep having babies."

Lost in memories, Odysseus wiped his tears with the back of his hand. "What a terrible place," he said. "I met all the dead heroes from Troy. And the ghost of Agamemnon, murdered by his own wife after he came home. He took me aside. Warned me to test my wife's loyalty before allowing myself to trust her." Odysseus pounded the earth with a clenched fist. "I won't even be safe in my own house! No matter how faithful Penelope might appear—"

"Teresias, did he talk of your route home?" I interrupted. I didn't want to hear one more word about Penelope. "Did he tell you about the island of Thrinacia?"

"Where the sun god's cattle live. He warned me we would be destroyed if we killed any of them."

"The god delights in his herd. He'll dash your ship to pieces if you so much as touch them."

"I won't go near the place," he said, impatient.

"It may not be easy to avoid. The truth is, you have only a chance of reaching home. I can point out some pitfalls along the way. For once, be quiet and listen to superior wisdom."

He had to think about that. "All right," he said, returning my smile.

"First you'll come to the Sirens, a band of beautiful women who inhabit a treacherous shoal where they sit combing their golden hair and singing their haunting songs. Any man who hears their clear-toned singing will lose all reason and steer his ship onto the rocks. They will sing to you of your glorious victory in Troy. They will appeal to your vanity."

His eyes sparkled with speculation.

"I'll give you beeswax from my hives," I said. "Use it to plug the ears of every man onboard."

"What if I want to hear their praises?"

"I should have known. Tell your men to tie you to the mast, then. Be sure to say that if you threaten or plead to be released, they must add extra ropes."

"After that?"

"Beyond the Sirens you'll enter a strait that winds between overhanging cliffs, no more than a bow's shot between the two. On one side is the whirlpool

Charybdis. No one has ever survived it. You must hug the opposite cliffs; they're home to a monster called Scylla. She has six scaly necks topped with six hideous heads. Whenever a ship sails by, she pops out of her hole and grabs a meal with her claws."

I knew this monster well. I didn't tell Odysseus I had created her in a fit of jealousy. Scylla had once been a beautiful nymph, a rival for the affections of a sea god named Glaucus. I wanted him for myself, but he had eyes only for her, so I poured my potion into the mountain pool where she liked to bathe. Another of the love stories from my dark past.

"I'll fight her off if she attacks *my* men!"

"Listen, firebrand, she's immortal. When will you learn to submit to the gods? Don't waste time arming yourself. Row as fast as you can and stay away from Charybdis' boiling waters. Better to lose six men than your whole ship."

But I was thinking, Why am I giving advice? I should let them all drown. I should turn Penelope into a huge, hairy spider. . . . Still, I heard myself saying, "After that—if you survive—you'll come to the green island of Thrinacia. Tell your men to leave the cattle alone and eat only the food I've given you."

The last morning on the windswept beach, he held me as the sun cast our joined shadows across the sand. I kept my grief hidden. But he was afraid to look at my eyes and went to his ship without once glancing back.

I sent them off with a stiff breeze and billowing sails; they needed only the steersman's hand to speed them on their way. I stayed there breathing the salt air, watching his ship cut the waves. Silhouetted against the pale blue morning, Odysseus waved a hand at me.

I'd always known he would leave me to complete his journey. I'd thought his time with me would be an entertaining interlude, that I was too powerful to be hurt. I was wrong. Even as I laughed at mortals for their foolish attachments, I had succumbed to the same folly. I had grown fond of this man.

I would not die of love. I tasted the sorrow on my tongue and wondered how I would live.

PART III

PALLAS ATHENA'S STORY:
A GODDESS INTERCEDES

CHAPTER 1

~

Knowing in advance the tragic outcome, I watched Odysseus's men feast on the sun god's cattle after they'd taken refuge on the island of Thrinacia. Having survived both Scylla and Charybdis, they had run short of food and ignored their captain's warnings, poaching three of the best bulls while Odysseus was up on the mountain praying for favorable winds.

Only Odysseus, who ate none of the meat, escaped the god's wrath. Clinging to the keel of his wrecked ship, he eventually washed up on the shores of another lonely goddess, this one a lovesick nymph named Kalypso. And, unlike Circe, she had no qualms about keeping a man against his will.

Odysseus begged to be allowed to construct a raft and sail home to Ithaca. Kalypso locked up all construction tools and forbade her servants, on threat of death, to aid him in this enterprise. He was an adequate bed partner, but the passion was all on her side. Still, for seven years she kept him in her lavishly furnished cave—at least at night. Poor soul, he spent his days sitting on the beach staring out at the endless ocean, his hopes of ever seeing his beloved Ithaca fading away.

Toward the end I watched, invisible, as Kalypso exhausted her persuasive arts. She told him she was more beautiful than Penelope, taller and fuller breasted. This superiority Odysseus conceded at once, but it didn't make him love her. She reminded him that Penelope would grow old and wrinkled— was already old—while she herself would forever wear the flush of youth. He responded that he would give his life for one hour with his wife.

At length Kalypso offered him immortality if he would consent willingly—and with a great deal more enthusiasm—to be her husband.

That's when I made up my mind to step in. Of all the mortals, Odysseus was my favorite. We'd fought side by side on Troy's wide plain, sending many a noble Trojan to the Land of the Dead. Beyond his skill as a warrior, I admired the man's grit, his ability to endure. And I loved his wiliness. A master of disguises, he could invent a story better than any man alive or dead.

He was not perfect; no mortal ever is. He could be headstrong, driven by the need to create his own legend. And if I had been content to stand aside watching these past nine years, it was, in part, because I was waiting to see if he would learn anything from all his trials.

When Odysseus turned down Kalypso's gift of immortality, I knew that his guile had matured into wisdom, that he had sailed in search of fame and found instead his own humanity. He'd learned that what he most cherished was what he'd left behind— on Ithaca.

The real obstacle to Odysseus's homecoming was not the nymph Kalypso, whose power was inferior to my own. It was my uncle Poseidon, who embraces the world with his oceans. And up on Mount Olympus, where the immortal gods make their home, there lived other relatives who'd supported the Trojans in the great war. My most dangerous adversary would be Aphrodite, goddess of love and beauty. The Trojan Paris had been her favorite, just as Odysseus was mine. One day when the battle was going badly for the Trojans, Aphrodite flew down to the field and fought beside him. Even got her robe dirty. Fighting alongside Odysseus, I nicked her with my spear. She yelled loud enough to wake the ghosts in Hades and ran away. Most amusing, but she'd never forgiven me, and she was sneaky.

Nevertheless, I thought I could persuade my father, Zeus Almighty, to intercede on Odysseus's behalf. The timing had to be right. I would have to wait until Uncle Poseidon made his annual journey to Ethiopia, which lies at the edge of the southern seas. Zeus would be more likely to act on my appeal during my uncle's absence—and when he returned, Poseidon wouldn't dare oppose his older brother's decision. Perhaps, when the time came, I could find a way to get rid of Aphrodite, too.

While waiting, I resolved to visit Ithaca and assess the situation there myself. I knew things were going badly for Penelope, that she was besieged by a wolf pack of suitors who refused to leave her halls. If I found Telemachus to be a true son of Odysseus, I would inspire him to stand up to these insistent bridegrooms.

I strapped on the golden sandals that transport me over the earth as fast as the wind, and soon stood on the island of Ithaca at the gate to the palace court-yard, disguised as a visiting merchant. We gods almost always take human form when we visit the mortals, either that or remain invisible. This allows us to observe what people are really up to.

The suitors in Odysseus's court were behaving badly, some throwing the discus, some playing draughts, sitting idly on skins of cattle they'd butchered and yelling out their bets. Two Ithacans were arm wrestling. A mainland warrior lay sprawled underneath their table in a puddle of red wine. This was an ordinary afternoon, not a feast day. These men should have been supervising servants or work-ing in their fields.

I recognized Telemachus, who came right away to greet me. He was beyond that gawky stage between boyhood and manhood, but still not quite comfortable with his long legs. Already taller than Odysseus, he had his father's fine eyes and full lips, and Penelope's chestnut brown hair. The beginnings of a beard shadowed his chin.

Only a slight stoop of his shoulders revealed the burden the young prince had been carrying. He took my spear, placed it in a weapons stand, then led me to a carved armchair. A servant poured water over my hands into a silver basin. A pretty maid brought meat and a basket of crusty brown loaves, while a herald kept my cup full of wine. Telemachus knew not to bother me with questions until I had eaten. I was pleased to see that even without a father's guidance, he knew how to observe the laws of hospitality.

While I ate, the suitors came swaggering into the hall and took what looked like their regular seats. Draping their cloaks on the benches, they shouted at servants to bring food and wine as if they were the hosts and not the guests.

Telemachus leaned closer to me. "I put you here in the corner so that their noise would not make you lose your appetite," he said, "but please, now that you've feasted, tell me your name and how you came here. Are you a friend of my father's?"

"Your father's and his father before that—I've heard old Laertes doesn't come to town anymore. My name is Nisus. I've come from Taphos with a cargo of bronze. And you must be Odysseus's son."

"My mother says I am."

"No one can witness his own begetting," I said, laughing. "But I assure you, you're Odysseus's son. You're very much like him."

A minstrel had begun to play. Some suitors were dancing and singing, while others shouted at them not to drown out the bard.

"What feast is this and who are these brawling guests?" I asked, knowing the answer but wanting to hear what the boy would say.

"Easy enough to dance," Telemachus muttered, "when someone else is paying for the food you eat. The truth is, all of them want to marry my mother. She'll have none of it, but they refuse to leave until she chooses one of them." He nodded at the bard. "Minstrels have come with news of all the heroes of the Trojan War—all except my father. We don't know if he's alive or dead. Yet here they stay, consuming our wealth."

"Outrageous! May Odysseus return and bring them instant death."

"The laws of hospitality require that we welcome guests."

"These same laws dictate that guests should leave when they're asked to."

"My mother has no power over them." The boy's face reddened in shame. "They laugh at me when I try to check their rowdiness."

"Listen, son, I'll pretend I'm your uncle and give you some advice. Tomorrow, call an assembly in the town square. As man of the house, it's time you appealed to the elders for help."

"Some elders are the fathers of these men. What if they mock me and refuse?"

"Then you'll know what kind of people you're up against—and what revenge they deserve."

He smiled, relishing the thought of revenge.

"After that meeting, whatever its outcome, get yourself a good ship—twenty oarsmen will do—and go find news of your father yourself! Go first to King Nestor in Pylos, but don't stay long. He'll bore you with speeches. Make haste to Menelaus in Sparta, who was last to return from the war. He's most likely to have heard something. I'm sure your father's a prisoner somewhere. If I know Odysseus, he'll find a way to get home."

Relief shone in Telemachus's eyes and then faded. No doubt he and his mother had been tortured by too many similar stories. The boy was determined to protect himself from further disappointment.

I placed my hand on his wrist, imbuing him with courage. "Telemachus, this is what your father would tell you if he were here in my place. Your boyhood days are over. Whatever has happened to Odysseus, it's time for you to do something about it."

He stammered his thanks, then said with sudden

determination, "You've spoken like a kind father. I'll follow your advice!"

I was about to leave, when Penelope came downstairs. She had aged well. A strand of silver graced her coil of braids, and her dark eyes held a wisdom born of suffering. The men quieted instantly, lusting after her with their eyes, all of them wanting to possess the wife of the great Odysseus. As such, she was a trophy to be won by the best among them. Of course, these men were also lured by her virtue, the fame of which had spread throughout the civilized world, and by her wealth, which they themselves were busy squandering.

Upstairs at her loom, she'd heard the bard in the hall below, singing of the heroes' return from Troy. Now tears filled her eyes as she addressed him. "Make an end to this song," she said. "I can't bear to hear the name of the place that took away my husband. Sing of other wars and other heroes. . . ."

My infusion of confidence must have taken effect, because Telemachus jumped to his feet, eager to impress the audience of suitors. "Don't blame our bad luck on the bard, Mother. Besides, my father was not the only one who didn't return. Many good men were lost and deserve to be remembered in song."

The suitors cast looks at one another, surprised at his bold words.

"Go see to your weaving," Telemachus ordered

with a dramatic gesture toward the stairs. "These are men's matters. A man rules this house now!"

Holding her veil to cover her smile, Penelope took her leave, secretly proud of her son's spirit. Clearly, Telemachus had been indulged by a devoted mother and an adoring nurse. I was sure neither of these women ever made a move to correct him. True, the boy showed good manners to strangers, but I would need to break him of such clumsy bravado. His prolonged adolescence was over. Telemachus would lack neither courage nor good sense by the time I was finished with him.

After I left the hall, claiming my crew was impatient for my return, a suitor named Eurymachus came over to Telemachus. "Who was that stranger and where did he come from?" he asked, pretending a friendly interest—and then, the question he really wanted to ask, "Did he bring news of your father?"

"Even if there had been news, I put no trust in such rumors," Telemachus said. "The stranger is called Nisus; he's chief to the Taphian people."

But in his heart I made sure the boy knew he'd been in the presence of a god.

When the singing and dancing grew more unruly, Telemachus climbed the stairs to his bedroom, the nurse Eurycleia lighting his way with a torch. Lost in thought, he took off his tunic and handed it to this good woman who'd cared for him since birth. She smoothed the fine linen before hanging it on a peg and shut the door softly behind her, just as she had done every night of his life and for his father before him.

Wrapped in sheepskins, the boy reflected on our meeting, giving himself completely to the course I had set for him. And when he dreamed, he already traveled the wide sea in search of his destiny.

CHAPTER 2

∾

Soon after dawn streaked the sky with her rosy fingers, heralds went throughout the town, calling the men to meet in the square. When Telemachus arrived, trailed by his two hounds, people murmured in praise, for I had graced him with beauty. The elders made room, and he took his father's seat in the assembly. One of them asked what public matter had brought them together, as no one had called an assembly since Odysseus had set sail for Troy nineteen years before.

Telemachus stood and a herald placed the speaker's staff in his hand. "This is a private matter I put before you," he said. "As you all know, my mother is besieged by insolent men who refuse to leave our halls. Some are seated here among us."

The suitors looked around, testing the mood.

"I'm addressing the fathers of these men, noble

citizens who fear the wrath of the gods. If you won't help me, I must conclude that *my* father was a cruel man who treated you badly—"

"It's your mother's fault!" the suitor Antinous interrupted. "She's been enticing us with the gifts Athena has given her—skill at handicrafts, a fine mind, and especially her womanly wiles. Send her to her father's house and have *him* arrange a marriage. But if she won't go, if she wants to go on teasing us, then we'll go on eating your sheep and cattle."

I was pleased to see Telemachus keep his courage and reply sensibly. "Antinous, I cannot turn my own mother out of the house. She wants no marriage. She wants to believe my father is alive somewhere."

"Odysseus is dead!" the bully Eurymachus shouted. "Would that you were dead along with him! We're not afraid of your warnings! We'll stay as long as she keeps putting us off!"

Though outraged at these brazen threats, I remained invisible as the elders exchanged eyebrow messages. Mentor, Odysseus's trusted captain, spoke into the heavy silence. "Do none of you remember Odysseus, who ruled us like a kind father? I call on you to protect his family! It sickens me to see the death of order in our kingdom. How can you sit and do nothing?"

Even Mentor couldn't move them to action. His fighting days were over, and no man dared oppose the powerful families that had sons and nephews among the suitors.

"Don't waste time appealing to their sense of honor," Telemachus told the old warrior. "These men have none. I have no more to say," he said, facing the elders. "I'm leaving for Pylos and Sparta to find out what happened to my father. All I ask is that you give me a ship."

Antinous grasped the boy's hand in mock congratulation. "Of course! We will gladly furnish you with a ship and the best of our oarsmen. How about some sacks of gold in the bargain?"

The suitors threw back their heads and laughed.

"I'll go to Pylos if I have to swim!" Telemachus yelled above their guffaws. "And when I return, I'll call upon the gods to grant retribution!"

Most of the crowd went on jeering, but Antinous spoke quietly to Eurymachus. "He may well bring back help from Sparta. Menelaus and Odysseus were close friends."

"There's been a change in the boy," Eurymachus said, eyes narrowed. "Did you hear how he talked last night in the hall?"

Antinous chuckled, pointing at Telemachus with his chin. "Who knows? The boy's ship could be lost at sea. He might meet with an accident just like his father did."

While the two were plotting Telemachus's murder, I inspired the boy to calm his rage and go alone to the seashore. There he washed his hands in the surf and offered prayers to the gods, to me in particular. The boy had guessed which one of us was working on his behalf. Still, I kept my identity hidden, and approached him this time in the shape of white-haired Mentor.

"Well done, my lad. You have your father's spirit after all. Go pack for your journey. I'll get us a ship and some volunteers."

Eyes sparkling with excitement, Telemachus ran back to the palace and found his nurse Eurycleia in the storeroom. "Nanny, I'm sailing tonight for Pylos to learn news of my father. I'll need a dozen kegs of wine and some skins of barley as soon as my mother has gone to bed."

She threw up both hands in horror. "Who put such a notion into your head? You're all your poor mother has left!"

"This is the gods' will, I'm certain of it! Promise you won't tell her till I'm gone. Otherwise, she'll be begging me to stay."

Meanwhile, disguised as Mentor, I went through the town asking for the ship and oarsmen, which people were willing to furnish. It was safer to help Odysseus's son in private than to speak up and offend certain families, especially Eurymachus's father, who was the wealthiest man in town.

Night fell. I summoned Telemachus, who supervised the loading of provisions into the hull. As the moon rose from the sea, I sat beside him on the stern and watched approvingly as he ordered the men to cast off the cables and hoist the white sail, which billowed out with a rippling West Wind that I provided to speed us on our way.

King Nestor knew nothing of Odysseus, but the visit to Pylos was good practice for Telemachus, who proved to be utterly ignorant of court protocol. As soon as we arrived at Nestor's palace, the boy suffered an attack of immobilizing shyness. "Mentor, I've never met a king," he whispered to me. "What can I say to him?"

Telemachus had many good qualities, but he had not inherited his father's gift of rhetoric. "You will think of something. The gods will put ideas into your head," I suggested pointedly, and he followed along behind me.

That night at the banquet in our honor, Nestor bored us with a windy story of how the gods had scattered the Greek fleet following a quarrel between Agamemnon and his brother Menelaus over which route to take home from Troy. After entertaining us for two days, Nestor was appalled when Telemachus tried to leave before receiving the ritual guest gifts, a two-handled silver cup and some richly woven blankets. The old king shook his head and looked over at me in obvious frustration.

I said, "It would perhaps be helpful, My Lord, if

you would send your son Peristratos to accompany
Telemachus on the trip overland to Sparta. The two
are of similar age, and he can set a good example,
schooled as he is in the affairs of court."

Nestor agreed immediately, and, later that day,
still posing as Mentor, I took Peristratos aside. "From
here on, it's up to you to teach the boy how to
behave. You've got your father's best chariot and
horses bred for speed. You two young bucks won't
want an old uncle slowing you down. I'll stay behind
and look after the ship."

Transporting myself ahead of them with my
golden sandals, I was able to observe their arrival in
Sparta, just as Menelaus and Helen were celebrating
the wedding of their daughter Hermione to the son
of the great Achilles. The two visitors were bathed
and then escorted to the hall, where the flash of
bronze and glitter of silver made Telemachus even
more tongue-tied than usual. King Menelaus himself
welcomed them. There was gray in his square-cut
red hair, but the burly, bowlegged warrior was still
solid as marble. As is customary, the king did not
ask their names before they had feasted. He himself
offered them a choice roast on a silver platter
trimmed with gold.

Telemachus sat turning his goblet, tracing the
engraved pattern with a finger. "Look at the ruby in
the base of this cup! It's so big, I can see myself in it,"
he said in an aside to Peristratos. "Look at the gold,

the amber and ivory! Zeus's palace on Olympus must look like this!"

Menelaus overheard. "Few rival me in treasures, most of it Trojan loot," he said. "But I would give it all in exchange for the men who never came home from that terrible war. Especially one of them, who still haunts my dreams." To their surprise, Menelaus launched into a description of Odysseus, his beloved comrade. "Surely they're all mourning for him at home—Penelope, old Laertes, and of course the boy. . . ."

At this talk of his own family, Telemachus could not hold back his grief. His shoulders shook with sobs; he covered his face with his purple cape.

"Come now," whispered Peristratos. "It's not fitting to cry over your meal."

Just then Helen came into the hall, still as beautiful as Aphrodite. Elbowed by Peristratos, Telemachus lifted his head.

Helen recognized the boy at once. *"Can it be?* You must be the son of Odysseus! I can see my cousin Penelope in you, too! How I have missed her all these years. Her hair was exactly that color. I can't believe you didn't recognize him," she said to Menelaus, who had leaped forward to sweep the boy off the floor in a crushing bear hug.

Telemachus was too overcome to respond, so Peristratos stood and bowed, introducing himself as the son of Nestor. "This is indeed Telemachus," he said. "My father sent me along as his escort. The boy has troubles at home and no one to stand up for him. He's here seeking news of his father."

Fortunately, both Helen and Menelaus had stories to tell of Odysseus's valor, giving Telemachus time to recover his tongue. Helen told of how Odysseus had disguised himself as a beggar to enter the Trojan citadel and learn their battle plans. She alone recognized him and helped him escape. "By then I was longing to come home," she said, with a sidelong glance at her husband. "I was sick at heart over the madness Aphrodite sent me, the way she tore me away from my husband and daughter."

I was tempted to materialize and ask her why—if she wanted so badly to return home—she hadn't simply escaped to the Greek camp with Odysseus.

But such logic would have been useless.

Like most humans, Helen blamed her catastrophic foolishness on us gods. It's something we laugh about up on Olympus. True, we are able to make their lives miserable, but most times, people have their own actions to thank for their bad fortune.

I was glad to see that Menelaus was not entirely convinced of her innocence, because he went on to tell of waiting inside the great horse with the other Greek warriors. After the Trojans had dragged it inside their walls, the hidden Greeks needed only to remain absolutely quiet until nightfall to launch their attack. "And during that endless afternoon,"

Menelaus said, "Helen walked around the horse, mimicking the voice of each man's wife—"

"I have no memory of this," Helen interrupted. "It must have been Aphrodite's doing."

Menelaus shrugged and continued. "All of us wanted to call out. Anticlus was just about to answer her, but Odysseus clamped his hand over the man's mouth. He saved our lives that day, and many others'."

In the month that followed, Menclaus and Helen treated Telemachus like their own son. Indeed, Helen was a blood relative, and Menelaus had no legitimate son of his own. Gradually the boy's awkwardness faded, and as he found his voice, his own plain-spoken wit emerged. My guidance was paying off. Telemachus learned to negotiate the complex gift-giving rituals, and the gifts were many. Helen gave him a robe for his future bride that she had embroidered with her own hands. Not to be outdone, Menelaus offered to send him home with three matched horses and a silver chariot.

"Please," Telemachus said, "let it not be horses. We have no wide roads or meadows. Ithaca's goat country, not horse country."

Menelaus ruffled the boy's hair. "You come of good stock to speak so frankly. Instead, I'll give you my most precious piece, a bowl with gold handles fashioned by the smith god Heiphaistos."

But Menelaus's most precious gift to Telemachus was not the wine bowl—it was the truth about Odysseus. During his travels, Menelaus had learned from an ancient sea god that Odysseus was alive and being held prisoner by the nymph Kalypso. This news, beyond all the lessons in kingship from his father's comrades, gave Telemachus the courage to return home.

I was satisfied with his progress. Telemachus had left Ithaca a boy and would return home a warrior who would do honor to his illustrious father. My work on earth was done for now. It was time to make my appeal at the Council of the Gods on Mount Olympus. My uncle Poseidon had begun his journey to the southern seas, and back in Ithaca, the suitors had just given me one more compelling argument for the release of Odysseus.

CHAPTER 3

❧

Throughout the travels on the mainland, I had kept an eye on events back in Ithaca. Penelope had been heartsick when she'd heard of her son's departure. But she soon received even more alarming news from the servant Eurycleia, who made it her business to know everything that went on in the men's hall.

At first the suitors assumed Telemachus was at his grandfather's farm or off with the swineherd, an old family retainer. When they found out the boy had really sailed for Pylos, they sent for the merchant who'd provided the ship, a man named Noemon.

"Did he take it against your will?" Eurymachus demanded.

"I offered it to Mentor," Noemon said. "There was something about him that could not be refused. *If* it was Mentor. I saw the old man in the square yesterday, yet I know he left here with Telemachus on the last full moon. Do you get my meaning, sir?"

So the suitors knew a god was at work. That put fear in their hearts, but it did not stop them. They resolved to sail their ship to a narrow channel between Ithaca and Samos and ambush the boy on his return.

This decision gave me my opening argument for the assembly of gods up on Mount Olympus. When it came my turn to speak, I told Zeus, "The suitors are going to murder Odysseus's son, Telemachus, who's gone to Pylos and Sparta seeking news of his father."

"My dear child," Zeus said, "you must go bring him back safely, for the boy has offended none of the gods."

"Father, can we also consider the case of Odysseus?"

Aphrodite twisted around to listen. She'd been admiring herself in a small hand mirror she always brought to relieve the boredom of council meetings.

"Can we not end his exile?" I asked. "When Telemachus returns to Ithaca, he'll need a father to protect him."

"Unfair!" Aphrodite tossed her head in my direction. "Athena's using her favorite daughter status to promote her favorite mortal."

I stared her down, eyes blazing. Though we were

both Zeus's daughters, there had never been any love between us. I said, "Just as you promoted Paris, who was much less worthy of our patronage."

Aphrodite was silent, searching for a way to convince our father, who had remained neutral during the great war. I didn't think she was smart enough to find one.

"Odysseus does not deserve our favor," she finally said. "Look what he did to Poseidon's son."

Zeus's expression remained noncommittal. In truth, the churlish Cyclops had few supporters on Olympus.

"Odysseus is guilty of the sin of pride," she said, flustered. "He sees himself as a god among men."

"He's spoken of as a god in songs and stories," I interrupted, "but he knows nothing of what the bards have been singing about him. In truth, he accepts his own humanity. Kalypso offered him immortality, and he turned it down."

Zeus nodded two or three times. "Go tell Kalypso our will: She shall release her prisoner and help him build a raft." Then, as he pointed a mighty finger at Aphrodite, he pronounced his decision. "Odysseus is fated to end his days at home."

My sister stomped out of the chamber. I thought that would be the last of her interference.

I went at once to inform Kalypso, who lives on Ogygia, at the navel of the world. So enchanting is this small island that the gods themselves marvel at its groves of sweet-smelling cyprus, its meadows of wild violets cut by winding streams. I found Kalypso alone in her cave. A fire of fragrant juniper flickered, its gold flames mirrored on the polished tile floor. Standing barefoot, she was working at her loom, her lustrous copper hair flowing down over her shoulders.

Kalypso saw me standing in the dappled shadows of a grapevine, which hung at the cave's entrance. "Athena, what an honor! You don't often pay me a visit. Come in, let me get you some refreshment."

I waved away her offer. "You have a man here, carried to you by the sea."

"Odysseus," she breathed, her eyes startled.

"Yes, Odysseus," I said. "Zeus orders you to send him home."

"How jealous you are up on Olympus! You're shocked when a goddess has a man in her bed, yet the gods take mortal women all the time!" She threw her shuttle to the floor. "All those years I waited for him to come. . . ."

"It is not his destiny to end his life here."

"I *love* him! I would have made him immortal!"

"Zeus *commands* you to let him go," I said, refusing to be drawn into a discussion of fairness.

"All right, he can leave!" She lifted her chin. "Let him take his chances at sea; I've no ships or sailors to offer."

"Kalypso, you would be wise to remember the wrath of Zeus Thunderer. If you refuse to help, you will face *his* punishment."

Even passion has its limits. She nodded and dropped her eyes.

"Where is he now?" I asked.

"Where else but down on the beach. He spends his life gazing out to sea."

"Then go speak to him."

I watched, unseen, as she went to execute her orders, coming up behind him on the beach. He jumped at her touch. "You needn't sit here grieving," Kalypso said. "I'm going to help you build a raft. I'll give you boiled meat and barley, and send you a fair wind."

Far from rejoicing, Odysseus just shook his head. "After all these years?" he said. "I fear you have something else in mind for me."

"Ah, Odysseus, you expect the whole world to be as crafty as yourself." She stroked his arm. "I'll swear a sacred oath to make no mischief against you. The gods on Olympus, who are stronger than I am, have declared that you should leave."

But her very name means "concealer," and her plotting was not over. She served a fine meal that night, and as they drank honeyed wine from silver goblets, she tempted him again with immortality.

"If you knew what terror awaits you on the sea and what troubles there are in Ithaca, you would stay here with me and accept my gift," she said. "Even Zeus cannot deny Poseidon his revenge."

When he refused, she tried another approach. "Come now, use your famous cleverness. Is Penelope more handsome than I am? It is dangerous for a mortal woman to rival a goddess in beauty," she added with a hint of warning.

Odysseus was clever enough to respond diplomatically. "Of course she could never rival you. Still, I long to see her. I'll take my chances, even if Poseidon wrecks me again."

The next morning she brought him a bronze ax and showed him a stand of pine trees, which he felled and trimmed. She supplied a boring tool to make holes for the lashings and cloth for the sail as well as plentiful stores of food and water. Finally, she warned him to keep the constellation of the great bear always on his left as he navigated toward Ithaca.

She did not go down to the beach to bid him farewell.

For seventeen days Odysseus sailed on smooth seas. But I hadn't counted on how long it would take to construct the raft. And in spite of all my efforts, my uncle Poseidon, who was even then on his way back from Africa, happened to spot his favorite victim. Uncle usually stayed away longer. I suspected Aphrodite; no doubt she went looking for him to tattle on me.

The sea god shook his blue mane and bellowed into the night, "As soon as my back is turned, Zeus changes his mind about Odysseus!" With his golden trident, Poseidon stirred up the waves and summoned all four winds. "Before this man touches land," he roared, "I will send him a storm straight out of Hades!"

Poseidon could not overrule his omnipotent brother, but he could still make trouble. And Odysseus was adrift in the sea god's element. Here, Uncle rules supreme, and I could do little to oppose him.

A huge surge rolled up, towering over Odysseus's raft. The mast snapped like a twig, knocking him overboard. My uncle held him under until he'd almost lost consciousness. Odysseus swam for his life and managed to scramble back onto the raft, which Poseidon then sent spinning up blue-black mountains and careering down watery cliffs until a gigantic swell curled up and smashed down, breaking apart the well-lashed planks. What remained of the raft climbed higher and higher up the curl of the next wave, while Odysseus clung to its side. Reaching the top, raft and rider were hurled into the black void.

Odysseus gulped the wet air before he went under again. I had lost sight of him for endless moments when his head broke the surface. Coughing and gasping, he lashed out for something to hold on to.

I couldn't stand to watch idly. With a quick sleight

of hand, I sent a piece of broken mast scudding toward him. He grabbed it and held on with all his waning strength. The screaming winds and towering waves punished him far into the night. Indeed, the all-enduring Odysseus was praying for death when he finally caught sight of land. Even then the coastline was rimmed by sharp reefs, ferociously pounded by Poseidon's angry sea. Odysseus didn't know it, but he'd reached Scheria, home of the Phaiakians, a peace-loving people much favored by the gods.

He swam along the reef, looking for a bay. At length he came to the mouth of a river, where, treading water, he prayed to the river god, "Have mercy. Save me from Poseidon's wrath!"

The river swept him into its embrace and propelled him toward the shallows. There Odysseus sank down on his knees, spitting up briny water. He had torn the skin from his hands climbing over the reef. His fingers were swollen, his eyes burning, his tunic had disintegrated. Never in his life had he felt so spent.

A less prudent man might have collapsed right there on the beach. Not my Odysseus. After he caught his breath, he stumbled to a stand of low trees overhung with vines. Concealed inside this natural bower, he scraped together a bed of leaves, heaping them over his body.

Still unseen, I poured deep, healing sleep upon him. Then I made my way to the palace of the Phaiakian King Alcinoos to engineer a proper welcome.

CHAPTER 4

❧

King Alcinoos had an only daughter, a green-eyed, tawny-haired girl named Nausicaa, who was the joy of his life. I drifted through spacious halls into her purple-bordered bedroom, where I entered her dream and urged her to take the family laundry down to the river at daybreak. Marriage had been much on the girl's mind, so I played into that interest. "It will be good for prospective bridegrooms to see you working and supervising servants," I told her, "a sign that you'll make a good wife."

At dawn she found her father already on his way to the council chamber and made her request.

"With five sons in the house, there's always a pile of dirty laundry," he said, patting her hand. "But don't exhaust yourself. Take the mule cart and have the servants pack a picnic hamper."

Not far from where Odysseus had come ashore,

Nausicaa and the dozen or so maids unloaded their cart and carried the clothes to the water, treading them into the sand, racing to see who could finish first. After the clean laundry was stretched on flat rocks to dry, they threw off their veils and began tossing a ball. Nausicaa, taller than all the others, sang a festival song as she led the game, her sun-bleached hair lifted by the breeze, her white arms flashing in the sun like a temple dancer's. When she threw the ball beyond the line of maids, it landed next to Odysseus's hiding place. The girls yelled for someone to get it.

Awakened by the noise, the naked Odysseus crawled out from underneath his tree. He broke off a leafy branch and, holding it over his manhood, he went toward the voices, propelled by hunger.

What a fright! A naked man, caked with sand, and striding toward them like a lion hunting a wild deer. The girls shrieked and scattered—all except the princess Nausicaa. I had taken her fear away.

After quickly deliberating, Odysseus was careful to keep his distance, to speak to her gently. "Are you mortal, fair maid? For I would liken you to Artemis, daughter of Zeus."

This flattery wasn't quite so outrageous as it may seem. Here was a girl of uncommon beauty, standing before him without her veil, ripe and blooming, desperately eager to fall in love.

"Wherever did you come from?" she cried,

laughing. "Our home lies so far from other lands, we almost never have mortal visitors."

"Poseidon cast me ashore here last night. Pity me, Queen," he said, clutching the leaves to his body. "Can you give me some rag to cover myself?"

This time his flattery *was* outrageous. Nausicaa was clearly too young to be a queen. I smiled to see Odysseus up to his old tricks.

"But, first, tell me what country this is," he said.

"This is the country of the Phaiakians. My father is King Alcinoos."

Nausicaa turned and scolded her maids, now peering out from behind bushes and trees. "Why do you run from this poor fellow? Zeus, god of strangers, would not approve. He sends us beggars and castaways, and we must gladly give what we can. Take him to the river, the sheltered spot where he can have a bath away from the wind. Climene, go find a dry tunic and one of my brothers' capes."

Stifling their giggles, the girls led Odysseus to the cove and prepared to bathe him. But he took the jar of oil from their hands, still holding tight to his branch. "Just stand back and let me wash the salt off," he said. "I'll rub myself with oil afterward."

Before Odysseus waded out of the river, I made him taller and handsomer, gave him a thick crop of curly, golden-brown hair, untouched by gray. He saw his reflection in the water's surface and smiled a speculative smile, knowing the gods were somehow working on his behalf.

He wasn't the only one to notice this transformation. Nausicaa stole a glance as he dressed in the clothes she'd left on a flat rock at the water's edge. "Look at him," she said to her maidens. "He wasn't much when we first saw him. Now he looks like one of the gods who rule the heavens."

"Ah, Princess, you're shopping for a husband," one of the maids teased.

"That's because none of the local boys are good enough for her!" another squealed, amid peals of laughter.

"I only wish I could have such a man, that he might choose to stay here with me. Hush, here he comes. Get him something to eat."

Nausicaa helped fold the clothes and pack them into the wagon. Then she went to where Odysseus was finishing his meal. "You seem a man of good sense," she said. "As long as we're out in the country, you can follow along behind the wagon. Before we reach the city walls, you'll find a grove of poplar trees and a fountain, sacred to the goddess Athena. Hide there and let us go up to the palace alone. . . ." She blushed, choosing her words. "If you came with me, people would talk. They'd say, 'Who is this handsome stranger with Nausicaa? Looks like a potential husband, some foreigner, or maybe some god who's come down from Olympus to answer her prayers. Seems only a god will do; she's turned up her nose at all the others.'"

The poor girl was hinting so broadly that no man could have failed to understand her invitation. I watched Odysseus carefully. Here was a ravishing young virgin—young enough to be his daughter—to keep him from his Penelope.

Odysseus took a steadying breath. "May the gods give you a fine husband, and may the two of you be of one heart," he said softly. "I have known such harmony with my own dear wife and could wish no better future for you."

She blinked and lowered her eyes. "You can ask anyone for directions to the palace," she said. "Come right into the great hall. Pass by my father's throne and kneel at my mother's feet. She'll be sitting next to the hearth carding purple yarn. If she approves of you, you'll live to see your native land . . . and your wife."

Nausicaa climbed into the cart and touched the mules with her whip, driving slowly so that Odysseus and the maids—now dancing along behind him and daring one another to tuck flowers into his hair—could follow on foot.

They reached my sacred grove just before sunset. Odysseus thanked Nausicaa and, after watching her leave, fell down on his knees to pray for his safe return. "Athena, give me some sign that you've come back to me," he said into the evening silence.

None came, and he got up and dusted off his knees. True, he suspected my intervention. But he didn't know I was right there, keeping out of sight, and that was just as well. I didn't want to provoke Uncle Poseidon until my protégé was home on Ithaca. A large patch of ocean remained to be negotiated.

Just as Odysseus was about to enter the city gates, I appeared in the guise of a young girl carrying a jug of water, and he asked me how to get to the palace. "You can follow me," I said. "First, let me give you some advice. Don't talk to anyone on your way. Our people travel the world in ships that fly as fast as a thought, but they don't take well to strangers in their own land."

To make sure he aroused no suspicion, I covered Odysseus with a sea fog, so no one could see him. He was free to marvel at the twin harbors, the well-crafted merchant ships, each one in its own mooring, the bustling market square and the high, curving palace walls.

"Here it is," I said. "Look for Queen Arete. Her husband honors her above all others. She has a fine mind and is skilled at mediating quarrels, even among men."

He thanked me and entered the royal compound, first passing through an orchard where all manner of trees bore fruit throughout the seasons, then crossing a spacious marble courtyard. Inside the great hall he was dazzled by jeweled floors, intricately painted borders, gold doors, and silver lintels.

Queen Arete sat beside the king, carding wool just as her daughter had described. She was a handsome, big-boned woman, with dark blond hair, and eyes that would smile easily. Just as Odysseus knelt before her, I lifted the mist that had covered his approach.

The guests in the hall fell silent, staring at this stranger who'd appeared from nowhere, knowing he must be protected by the immortals.

"Honored Queen, may the gods grant happiness to all who are feasting here," he said. "I come as supplicant. I beg you to take pity on me and send me back to the island of my birth. I've been away for nineteen years; I want to see my home before I die."

Queen Arete glanced at her husband, who rose and extended his hand to Odysseus. After seating him next to his own throne, the king signaled servants for food and wine. No one bothered the guest with questions while he was eating, but Alcinoos spoke of him to his assembled nobles. "Let's give this man the help he needs. Tomorrow morning we'll meet to talk about getting him home."

They all applauded this decision and raised their wine cups in a toast to Odysseus.

"Or if he is one of the immortals come down among us, we can talk about what that means for us," the king said, turning to Odysseus. "In the past, the gods have always visited us without disguise."

Odysseus shook his head. "I'm not one of the gods. I'm just a man, much afflicted by sorrows."

Heralds were circulating among the guests, refilling wine cups. According to the leave-taking ritual, each man poured a final libation onto the floor for the gods and departed, leaving Odysseus alone with the king and queen and servants clearing away the feast.

Arete leaned forward then to speak. "I'll ask my questions now that you've eaten. Who are you and where do you come from?" She pointed at his tunic. "And where did you get those clothes?"

Odysseus smiled sheepishly. Of course Arete recognized his tunic and cape. She'd woven the cloth for them herself.

"My Lady, I've been seven years on the island of Ogygia, where I was held captive by a nymph called Kalypso. Finally, she set me free, but Poseidon Earthshaker broke apart my raft, and last night I was thrown up on your shores. This morning I heard your daughter with her maids on the beach. I appealed to her; she gave me these clothes. She's very sensible for one so young."

"Not at all," Alcinoos said, frowning. "She should have brought you up here right away."

"Don't blame your daughter. She was afraid you might be angry to see her with a strange man."

"How could she have known our welcome would be friendly?" Arete said, touching her husband's wrist. She got up then and went to direct the maids to prepare a bed for Odysseus underneath the open gallery. Her first question—who was this visitor?—had not been answered, but Arete had the wisdom to wait.

Next morning the king called a council. "I need our best oarsmen to ferry this guest back to his homeland," he announced. Fifty-two volunteers and all the lords of the land were invited to a farewell banquet. Alcinoos sent for his bard and instructed servants to kill a dozen sheep and eight boars.

By afternoon the open galleries and all the court-yards were filled with revelers. The celebrated bard, Demodocos, was singing about a quarrel between Odysseus and Achilles during the last year of the war. The diners were enjoying themselves too much to notice, but the king, seated next to Odysseus, saw his mysterious guest trying to hide his tears.

Next the bard began a well-loved song about how Odysseus tricked the Trojans into thinking the huge wooden horse that the Greeks left behind was a sacrifice to the gods. Odysseus had never before heard songs of his adventures with his beloved comrades. Now he wept openly.

Alcinoos called out, "Stop the song, our guest is troubled by it!" And then, to Odysseus, he said, "Did one of your kinsmen die in that war? Perhaps a dear friend?" The king smiled encouragement. "The time has come for you to tell *your* story, who you are and where you come from."

Odysseus wiped his tears and looked at the faces of his hosts. I spoke a thought into his mind: "You must let down your guard and trust the kindness of these strangers."

"I am Odysseus, son of Laertes," he said with a long sigh, "the same Odysseus who waited inside that great horse with my warriors. Since that time, the gods have given me more than my share of troubles." He had to pause while his audience gasped in surprise. "I come from the island of Ithaca. It's a rugged land, but to me, the most beautiful place on earth."

Then the bard set down his lyre, and the world's greatest storyteller launched into his own story, leaning forward, savoring that power he could still hold over an audience. Grown men cringed as he described the blinding of Polyphemus, the fiery lakes of Hades, the waterspouts of Charybdis. They marveled at the Lotus-eaters' magic fruit and the Sirens' deadly song, which Odysseus alone had lived to tell about. And all through the afternoon he told of the monsters and of the women who had loved and protected him.

"But they never had my heart," he told them, remembering Circe and Kalypso. The story worked its magic on the teller as well, for as he relived the wonders of his journey, Odysseus understood that he was ready to return with a full heart to the simple life on Ithaca. It was deep night when he finished; his listeners in the great hall sat spellbound as the silence pooled around them.

Alcinoos rose then from his throne. "Such entertainment deserves a reward!" he said. "I charge each man here to offer a bronze tripod or cauldron and each a nugget of gold to cement our friendship with the king of Ithaca."

The noblemen agreed joyfully and sent their heralds to collect the gifts. Queen Arete provided a carved chest, inlaid with silver, for the treasures. When preparations for Odysseus's departure were complete, the king spoke to his guest alone. "There is such love between us, I only wish you would cancel your journey and stay here. Our daughter has taken such a fancy to you. . . ."

Here was the offer I had been expecting. I waited.

"If you become my son-in-law," Alcinoos was saying, "I will give you a great house and a fine estate."

Would Odysseus pass this final test? He was silent a moment, and I saw that he was struggling to find a tactful way to decline the offer.

Alcinoos, ever the sensitive host, patted his shoulder. "Never mind, I can tell your heart is set on going home," the king said. "May you return to Ithaca to find your wife and family safe."

Odysseus embraced both the king and the queen and left the hall. But there was one more farewell waiting for him—Nausicaa, her face pale in the shadows of the vestibule. I admired the girl's courage. Her father would punish her for being there, unveiled, unchaperoned, seeking words with a male guest.

"I came to wish you a safe voyage," she said, her voice tremulous, and then, "Will you remember me when you're back home with your wife?"

Odysseus reached to take her hands, but thought better of it. She was so young, so vulnerable, lusting after something more than her secure world but not at all sure what that was. He said, "If Zeus will allow me to return home, I will remember you always in my prayers. Nausicaa, dearest girl, you gave me back my life!"

I knew then that Odysseus was truly ready to go home, and I was gratified.

He passed out of the palace compound and, accompanied only by heralds carrying his gifts, went down to the ship. The crew had prepared a bed of fleece on the stern, where Odysseus stretched out under a canopy of stars. The oarsmen took their places; the captain called out the rhythm of the strokes. Once clear of the harbor, they hoisted sail, and the ship surged across the water, its full sails like the wings of a great bird. Not even the soaring hawk could have kept pace with her.

Odysseus missed this final marvel, however. I had granted him a sleep so deep and so delicious that he didn't even stir when the ship beached in his favorite harbor on seagirt Ithaca. Carefully, they wrapped him in blankets and carried him to shore, after which they stacked his treasures underneath an olive tree, so that he would see them as soon as he awoke.

CHAPTER 5

~

J ust before Odysseus opened his eyes, I spread a thick mist over the island.

"Traitors!" he yelled, scrambling to his feet. "They promised to ferry me to sunny Ithaca, and they've delivered me to still another foreign land!"

He groped about in the sand and located the gold nuggets, bronze tripods, the herb-scented robes. Finding the gifts softened his anger at the Phaiakians. Still, he didn't know he was at last on his own shores until I came along, disguised as a shepherd boy, and he asked me what land this was.

"You really don't know? Stranger, this is the island of Ithaca. Its fame has reached all the way to Troy."

Odysseus curbed his racing heart and answered calmly. "Yes, I have heard of Ithaca, even as far away as Crete." Taking my measure with his shrewd eyes, he began a story of having been exiled from Crete for killing the king's son in a fight.

I had to smile. "Odysseus, you're still the world's champion liar. Can't you abandon your tricks now that you're home? No, I'm not scolding. Of all the mortals, you're most like myself. We're both famous for our wiles." I revealed myself then in my true form, a goddess, tall and serene, with laughing gray eyes. "Ah, now you recognize me!"

As usual, the rascal didn't show the proper reverence in the presence of an immortal.

"It's not easy to know you with all the shapes you take," he said. "But I wasn't convinced by the shepherd boy; he was too elegantly dressed. Tell me, is this really Ithaca?"

"Always so wary." I lifted my hands, and the gray mist rolled back. "Look, your favorite bay! See the nymphs' cave?"

Eyes shining with tears of joy, he knelt and kissed the fruitful earth. "Thank you, Athena. I owe great sacrifices to you, and to Father Zeus," he said. "It's just as I left it, and Athena once more at my side, just as when we fought together outside the walls of Troy!" And then, glancing up, he said, "You were so good to me then. Why did you desert me?"

"I couldn't offend my uncle Poseidon, who was furious at you for blinding his favorite son." This was not the whole truth; we gods do not reveal all our secrets, even to our favorites. I said, "Zeus has given permission for me to help you take back your home. Let's hide your treasures inside the cave, and make plans."

As we stowed away the Phaiakians' gifts, I told Odysseus of the suitors' insolence and of Telemachus's journey to meet the mainland kings. And still this man was questioning my divine judgment!

"Why didn't you just tell Telemachus yourself of my whereabouts?" he said. "Why subject the boy to the dangers of the open sea?"

"You've no cause for alarm," I answered, eyes flashing. "I took Telemachus to Pylos and Sparta myself. I wanted him to gain respect abroad. Even now he sits in the splendid court of Menelaus, surrounded by gifts, worthy of his famous father."

He smiled apologetically.

I said, "True enough, some of the suitors have hatched a plot to ambush him on his return, but I don't think that will come to pass."

Odysseus surveyed the rocky hillside. "I'll need a place to hide while I look things over."

"That's why you're my favorite. Any other man would be running up to the palace to embrace his wife, maybe getting himself killed in the bargain. You can go to Mentor; the old soldier's done his best for your family."

"Mentor's too close to town. There's a man called Eumaeus, foreman to the herdsmen on this side of the island."

"The swineherd."

"Yes, but from a noble family, stolen into slavery. My mother raised him like her own child. He'll be loyal if he's still alive. . . . Immortal gods, almost twenty years!" Odysseus studied the curve of beach, the mountains rising above, as if willing himself to believe he was really home. "A good man, Eumaeus," he said finally. "Used to dote on Telemachus. Still, I'll have to test him first."

I nodded approval. "Tell no one. Trust no one. I'll see to it that you won't be recognized." With the touch of a finger, I transformed him into an old man, skin wrinkled and spotted, back bent, his once thick hair reduced to silver strands across a bony skull.

"That should keep the women away from you for a while," I said, laughing. "I'll leave you now and go fetch your son from his mission."

I watched him climb the hill to Eumaeus's hut, breathing in the wild oregano, filling his eyes with the rocky landscape.

The swineherd came running when he heard his watchdogs barking at a filthy beggar approaching on the path.

"Off with you, Zanthos! Down, Skylos!" Eumaeus yelled at the dogs. "Father Zeus would punish you for harming a visitor who seeks hospitality. There, that's a good dog. Just let him sniff your hand," he said to the beggar. "Come, I'll give you bread and wine; you can tell me how you came to our accursed island. . . ."

Eumaeus gave quick proof of his loyalty as he led

the way to his hut. "There's a day, long ago, more than five hundred pigs we kept, for trading and for our lord's table." He gestured to the twelve styes he'd built, the rock walls he'd fashioned, each stone fitted carefully into place. "Then my master, King Odysseus—so fine a man, he has no equal—went off to fight in the Trojan War. Distinguished himself, he did. A prince among men!" Eumaeus spit on the path. "He's dead now. Would that Helen had died, too. A curse on that woman, she's the start of all our troubles. Here, come inside, old-timer, careful of the stone sill. It's not much, but you're welcome."

Odysseus had paused in the doorway and was looking up at Mount Neriton, its slopes clad in shimmering greenery. "You've heard no news of him, then, your king . . . Odysseus?"

"Stories, yes. The cruelest of lies torturing our poor queen." Eumaeus clucked his tongue. "If our master's not dead, he's begging for scraps in some foreign port, while I'm fattening his hogs for wastrels to eat. My herd is down to less than fifty."

The swineherd piled branches for a seat and covered them with sheepskins. "Sit here, Granddad. Have you only just landed? Surely you've heard what's happening up at our palace? I can't bear to go there anymore. Not unless my lady calls for me, but she stays hidden in her rooms. Can't stand the sight of the troublemakers eating up our stores, carousing all day and all night."

"I've heard of Queen Penelope. What keeps her from choosing the best of the suitors and preserving her son's legacy?"

"*Because she wants no other man!* But it may come to that; that's her dilemma. She may have to pick one of the brutes to protect her boy." He lowered his voice and leaned closer. "Odysseus's only son, Telemachus, went off to Sparta looking for news of his father. Who knows what got into him, leaving without a word? A good, sturdy boy, but untried in battle. Worried sick about him, I am. Even now, the louts could be waiting for him at the entrance to the bay. May the gods protect him!"

"If he's such a man as you say his father was, you might expect some help from the gods."

"Who can tell? Their ways are too mysterious for my poor brain. Enough bad news. I'll get you some food—all that's left; the good cuts have gone to the gluttons up at the palace." He passed a basket of bread to his guest. "So tell me, Granddad, what are you called? Where did you come from?"

Odysseus broke apart one of the loaves. "Ah, that's a story. I could go on for years and not reach the end of my troubles."

This time Odysseus pretended to be the bastard son of a Cretan nobleman who'd been kidnapped by Egyptian pirates. His tale—full of adventures and misadventures—lasted until nightfall. All the young herdsmen had returned from the fields and were gathered around in enraptured silence. Odysseus's Cretan had just survived the Trojan War when Eumaeus fixed a bed of sheepskins and handed the guest a blanket. "Meaning no disrespect," he said, "but we're up at dawn here to take care of the pigs. It's high time we enjoyed the boon of sleep."

Two days later Odysseus and Eumaeus were eating breakfast when I returned with Telemachus, whose ship I'd propelled in record speed, cutting a swath around the headland where the suitors lay hidden. Posing as Mentor, I accompanied the boy on his return and left him at the harbor with instructions to seek news at the swineherd's hut. Then I followed, invisible, as Telemachus bounded up the path. When he reached Eumaeus's compound, the dogs raced to greet him with joyful yelps.

"Listen," Odysseus said inside the hut, "here's someone the dogs know well."

Peering from the doorway, Eumaeus dropped the bowl he'd been using to mix wine. *It's Prince Telemachus!* The dogs love him just as I do! Stranger, you've brought us luck!" Eumaeus threw back his head, stretching both arms to the sky. "Zeus Cloudgatherer, we owe you a great sacrifice!"

Odysseus stood in the doorway, shading his eyes against the sun. He watched Eumaeus reach up to embrace a well-built young man, taller and leaner than himself but with his own hazel eyes and high cheekbones. The boy's dark hair was shot with the same reddish highlights as Penelope's had been that first day in the orchard.

The swineherd was sobbing and planting kisses on the boy's face while the two dogs circled his feet, barking. "Immortal gods, I thought you were lost to us!" Eumaeus cried. "You know they were planning to ambush you?"

Telemachus wrapped a playful arm around the older man's neck. "All right, Uncle, I'm here! With good news, too. But, first, run and tell my mother I'm back. I don't want to cause her any more grief. Find out what's happening up there. Has she decided to marry one of the villains?"

"Not *her*! She'll have none of them. She's still waiting and pining, weaving away the days and weeping away the nights. What about your grandfather, old Laertes? He's taken almost no food since you left. Should I go up to the farm?"

"Come right back. Mother can send Eurycleia to tell him the news."

"Aye, Master. There's a visitor inside the hut, an old seafaring man. He'll see to your breakfast. No harm to him."

Eumaeus rushed inside to strap on his sandals, calling out to Odysseus, "Grandpa, see the boy gets wine and bread. Tell the men to slaughter our fattest porker. To hell with them up at the palace! We'll make a proper sacrifice when I get back." Then he was trudging up the path toward town.

"Uncle! Tell no one that I'm here! Only my mother!" the boy yelled after him.

I came up behind Odysseus at the entrance to the hut. "Look at his loose stride," I said. "He walks just like you do. Look at his beard."

I was invisible, but Odysseus knew well my voice. Still, he didn't answer. The wonder of his child's manhood stunned him, and he stayed rooted in the doorway, tears streaming down his cheeks. "Athena," he finally whispered, "give me leave to tell him who I am."

"Yes, of course, he must be part of our revenge."

Like a man sleepwalking, Odysseus stepped out into the sunshine. And as his beloved son drew near, this world-famous storyteller was, for once in his life, speechless.

I said, "Go ahead, you can touch him. He's real." I gave Odysseus back his glowing tan, a full thatch of hair, and gold-tinged beard. I firmed his jaw and restored him to his full height.

Watching this transformation, Telemachus halted just inside the stone wall. He couldn't see me standing behind his father, but the dogs sensed my presence, cringing at his feet.

"What magic is this?" Telemachus cried out. "Who *are* you, stranger? I know not what god I'm in the presence of, but we'll sacrifice a heifer with horns of gold. Just be merciful—"

"I'm not a god, Telemachus, I'm your father."

It was as if Odysseus had reached out and slapped him. "*Don't say that!* A moment ago you were old and wrapped in rags. Now look at you! Look at your fine cloak! Only a god could produce such changes!"

"I know about the suitors," Odysseus said in a tone of apology, "about all the hardships you've endured."

"Why do you trick me? What joy is there in tormenting a mortal who has no power to match your own?"

"It's true that Athena, my helpmate, altered me so I would not be recognized. Just now, she's given me back my former appearance so that you could know me. It's *her* power that makes me young or old, not mine."

Tears pooled in the boy's eyes.

"I'm not one of the immortals. Dear Telemachus, can't you see your own features mirrored in my face?"

And still the boy resisted, stepping backward on the path, his jaw clenched, his bronze spear held stiffly in front of him.

"Look at me, son. This is the only father you'll ever know. Here I am, just as you see me. I've come home after endless wanderings." Odysseus swallowed hard. "And I will never leave you again."

With a choked cry the boy dropped his spear and stumbled forward, falling into his father's arms. The two clung together and sobbed, their wails echoing from the mountains like the cries of eagles.

Telemachus was first to pull away, overcome by the need to know. "Where have you been, and how did you get back?" he asked, crying and laughing at the same time. "I know you didn't come here on foot."

"I was brought home by the Phaiakians, a noble race who live almost like gods."

"Menelaus told me you were held prisoner by the nymph Kalypso."

"Son, it's a long story, one I can spin for you all the nights to come. For now, I need to know what we're up against, how many suitors. We'll talk while you eat. The swineherd has put me in charge of breakfast."

Inside the hut, sitting cross-legged on sheepskins, Telemachus listed the men from different islands and mainland towns. "Fifty-two from Dulichion alone. Twenty from Zanthe. Twelve high-ranking lords from Ithaca." He passed a hand over his brow. "Think, Father, are none of your loyal shipmates left to fight beside us? I'm not afraid of battle, but how can we take them on, just the two of us?"

Odysseus chuckled. "Just the two of us? We'll have Athena, goddess of war, fighting alongside. She's blazing for a good battle. Here's the plan. When Athena gives the signal, I want you to round up the weapons in the great hall. Just leave a pair of swords and spears for the two of us."

Telemachus smiled, imagining the fighting.

"It's time now to visit the palace. And for that, I'll have to ask Athena to restore me to my former shabbiness." He was silent a moment. "One more thing. Tell no one I'm here. Not even your mother."

"I fear for you, Father. These men will show no kindness to an old beggar."

"I'm no stranger to insults and blows. Let them carry on in all their insolence. Even if they drag me by the heels, make no move to protect me—"

"How can I stand by and see you insulted?"

"You'll hold on to your rage. Cherish it. Trust me, son, anger makes the best fighters. After all their wooing, it will be a blood wedding they'll have. Come, let's be off. I'll follow behind you."

It was a joy to see father and son working together, but I would have to keep close watch. Telemachus was already marked for murder. And if the suitors for an instant suspected who this beggar was, his life would be forfeit before even I could defend him.

❖ PART IV ❖

EURYCLEIA'S STORY:
AN OLD SERVANT
RECOGNIZES HER MASTER

CHAPTER 1

ꝏ

May the gods forgive me, I didn't know my master. Disguised he was as a raggedy graybeard, bent over, leaning on a stick, with no hair on his head and no meat on his shanks.

"Just what we need, one more useless mouth to feed." More's the shame, that's what I said to the serving girls when I first saw him. No surprise it was to see the boy helping an old beggar. Telemachus was always bringing home strays. Such a sweet boy, not a rascal like his father. That one kept me running when he was a babe. But I was young then, and Odysseus could always charm me out of a spanking.

I didn't notice how carefully the boy was settling the old codger next to the double doors that led to the great hall. Too excited I was seeing my Telemachus alive. We knew he was safe, mind you. The swineherd came that morning with the news, and my lady sent me running to the farm to tell old Laertes. Poor man, such hardship he's suffered, and none of it deserved.

So much happening at once, I'm botching the telling of it. Zeus be praised, this was the best day of my life. Let me think how it all went. I just got back from Laertes' farm, and there was my boy with his beggar. The louts were too busy sucking up wine and throwing javelins. They didn't even notice.

"Almighty gods!" I sobbed. "Look, maids, the young master's come home!" I dropped my basket and ran to give my precious boy a hug.

"Enough, Nanny, you're crying all over my tunic." Telemachus grinned, pushing me away. "And lower your voice."

"Don't give *me* scoldings, I can still take the likes of you over my knee."

"Not when I've brought you a new robe from Sparta. Menelaus and Helen loaded me down with all sorts of gifts!" So proud of himself he was. "They're hidden away for now," he said. "Wait till you see all my treasures."

"No need to whisper, they're all too drunk." I pointed at a scoundrel called Antinous, who was arguing with another villain called Eurymachus over his throw in the game of draughts, the other fools yelling out their bets so loud, you couldn't have heard Zeus's thunderbolts.

"Run upstairs to your mother," I said. "Made herself sick with worry, she did. I'll take care of your guest." I looked down at the beggar. Something wrong here, I thought, a kind of dignity that shone through the rags. I can say that now, mind you, but the disgrace is still mine that I didn't know my master for who he was.

"Yes, Nanny. She'll never stop crying till she sees me in the flesh. Get the old man some wine, but don't call attention to him."

Too late for that. Before I could get back with the wine, Eurymachus spotted him. You'd think the louts could ignore a poor beggar sitting in the courtyard not bothering anyone. That tells you what kind of trash was there tormenting my lady.

"Who's that filthy leech next to the door?" Eurymachus called out. "Why are you serving him, woman? He belongs in the pen with the swine, not ruining our day with his foul smells."

"Odysseus never refused a man in need," I said. "How many of your fathers came to our king for protection? Did he ever turn away the hungry or treat any man with disrespect?"

They laughed at me. "Woman, over here! More wine!" Antinous shouted.

Let him throw something at me, the brute. I'm not afraid. I poured wine in a silver cup and passed it to the beggar. Antinous grabbed one of the stewards by the neck and growled his order into the boy's face. "Every time I look at them I want to chop heads," I said to the beggar.

"Zeus will punish them in his own good time," he answered in a voice that was too rich and deep for an old man. And still I didn't recognize him.

But Odysseus's old hunting dog, Argos—he was sleeping in the corner on a heap of rags—picked up his ears and sniffed the air. Had I known that dog was hearing his master's voice after nineteen years, I would have broken down weeping right then. Old Argos was a sad sight, with milky eyes and mangy patches where he'd scratched his skin raw. He croaked a feeble bark, wagged his mangy tail. Started off walking—got almost all the way to Odysseus—then dropped down, head on his paws, and closed his eyes.

"Poor creature," I said, "doesn't get around much. Spends his days sleeping."

The beggar turned away. I thought I saw him wipe his eyes. "I like dogs," he said. "I can tell that your old hound once had fine lines." He went and knelt beside the dog. Telemachus came back then, and the two exchanged a look.

"He's dead, your father's old hunting dog," the old man said. "I'll go bury him in the garden."

Eyes glistening with tears, Telemachus knelt beside him. "Let me do it," he said after a while.

Having visions, I was. I saw the two of them back before the war. Master in his leather vest, Argos fast and sleek, out for a morning hunt. Never a deer could outrun him, such a tracker he was. I saw the hound darting and weaving, nose to the ground, Odysseus racing behind. . . .

"Don't cry, Auntie," Telemachus was saying. "Argos was old, very old for a dog."

"'Tis true, of course. Still, I had this foolish notion he was hanging on to see his master one more time before he passed. Pay no mind to a silly old woman." I wiped the tears on my sleeve. "What says your mother?"

Telemachus glanced over at the suitors. They still hadn't noticed him. "She wants to meet our guest."

"Every visitor comes in from overseas, she's fishing for news," I said to the beggar. "So many sightings in the years since the war, and each time her poor heart breaks all over again. Useless to talk her out of it; she'll do anything for a word about the master."

The beggar pointed with his chin at Eurymachus. "Better to wait until they've gone off to their beds. Tell your mother she can bring down her favorite chair then."

Something tugged at my memory. How could the old man know about my lady's chair that my lord ordered for her when she came here as a beautiful bride?

"Tell her I'll answer her questions about her husband when we can talk in private."

"I'm sure she'll see the sense in waiting," Telemachus said. "For now, Mother wants to offer you clean clothing and a bath."

"Thank you, but no; I'm used to a rough life."

"At least allow my old servant to wash your feet."

"Very well," the old man said. He glanced up at me, shading his eyes from the sun. The two knelt a moment longer while the beggar stroked the dog's grimy head. "Go ahead, you can take him," he finally said, and Telemachus lifted the body and went off.

Truth be told, I wasn't happy to wash the filthy feet of a filthy beggar, but I knew my boy meant to show the proper hospitality. I went grumbling to get a basin of water. When I came back, it took a while to settle my old bones at the beggar's feet. Then I began sponging away the dirt. My hands are not as strong as they once were, but I could still give a proper massage to his calves. That's when I felt the scar. My hands fumbled with his rags as I traced it with my finger. A crescent shape it was, going down from the knee. A wild boar gave it to Odysseus when he was still a fearless boy.

"Master!" I breathed.

I dropped his foot. The bronze basin clattered to the floor, water sloshing all over the place. I was thinking, Almighty gods, how the years have aged you! What a terrible thing it is to grow old. "Zeus Thunderer," I said, my voice choking in my throat. "I didn't know you!"

Swift as a mountain lion, he sprang forward and

covered my mouth with his hand. "Nanny, do you want to get me killed? You're not to tell anyone. Not even Penelope."

I pushed aside his hand. "But, My Lord, she's waited so long!"

"I could always count on your common sense; I count on it now."

"For shame," I said. "You think you have something to fear from *her*? That she could want one of these ruffians?"

He tightened his grip on my arm, looking at me from under his brows, a look I remembered well. "You'll tell no one till I'm ready to take back my hall. The boy knows, and now you. Tomorrow we'll tell the swineherd and Mentor. That's all."

When I returned with a full basin, the hall was dead quiet. Telemachus was coming back into the courtyard, and the suitors were all staring, their stupid mouths hanging open.

"They've finally seen him," Odysseus said softly. "Probably wondering what happened to the ship they sent to ambush him."

The men were giving each other eyebrow messages. At a nod from Antinous, they all got up and went stomping out the gate.

I stared daggers at them, cursing their eyes, wishing them all in the Land of the Dead. "Villains," I said. "Off to make another plan to murder my boy."

"Yes, Nanny, but Athena is watching, and she

wants vengeance as much as we do. She's the one who's altered my appearance so I would not be recognized."

"Athena won't mind a little help," I said. I ran to the pantry and sent a loyal slave to go listen to their talk. He hid behind a wall when Antinous gathered the men in the garden, and reported the doings back to me.

"We'll drag Telemachus to the fields and murder him before he calls the elders to another council," Antinous had told them. The scoundrel was afraid the townspeople would take up weapons for Telemachus, so radiant the boy looked, confidence shining from him like beams from the sun's chariot.

Later that morning I sacrificed to Father Zeus. It wasn't what I would have wished—a heifer with gilded horns. All I had was some white barley and a jug of our best wine. But I bathed my face and splashed water on my wrists, proper like.

"It's a miracle you're giving us," I said. "We thank you, the boy and me. My lady would be here on her knees, too, if only she knew. For years, Lord, I've been staying alive, hauling my old body out of bed on the chance that my master might come back to us. Now he's home, gods be praised. I know Bright Eyes Athena is here by his side. But, Heavenly Father, a hundred seasoned warriors against a father and son?"

I slowly poured the libation of wine onto the

stone surface of the altar. If Zeus was listening, I wanted those odds to sink in. "You remember Odysseus, that man who saved you the thighs of his best prize bulls? Who never failed to honor his gods?" I took a breath and let it out slowly. "Mighty Zeus, ruler of heaven and earth, help Master rid us of the vermin infesting our home."

And walking away, I said one more silent prayer: *And make Odysseus tell his wife that he's home at last. My lady won't forgive us for shutting her out of this final battle.*

CHAPTER 2

❧

The louts came back in time for the noon meal, full of their plans. No surprise, mind you. I never knew them to miss any of the free food.

No small job it is, feeding a hundred worthless mouths. To see it done proper, I had to be in ten places at once; it means dishonor to our house if it's not done proper. Master would see I could still run a household, even with my hair gone all white. I kept them hopping, each servant in his place and no dilly-dallying—stewards mixing and pouring wine, house-maids carrying baskets of bread from the oven, carvers cutting meat for pages to deliver to the tables. The real preparation starts at dawn, with twenty slaves grinding barley from morning to night. But enough about food. I'm getting away from my story.

While the suitors were gorging themselves and

guzzling their wine, Telemachus brought Odysseus a sack and told him to go around the hall begging for dinner. Turns out that was part of the plan. Athena wanted to see if there were any gentlemen among them. I could have told her there were none.

Some of the louts were surprised to see the beggar. Wanted to know who was this man. Melantho, a serving woman of ours who was always fawning on that bully Eurymachus, she told them Telemachus found him in town near the fountain. Always pretending like she knew everything, that one.

"Don't we have enough beggars?" Eurymachus groaned.

Even so, all gave a scrap of food, some with pity, some with an insult, all except that blackhearted Antinous. When it came his turn, he told Odysseus to get out of his sight and be quick about it.

"You're such a father figure to me, Antinous," Telemachus said, sarcastic like. "I can always look at you and learn how to be a man. Go ahead, give him something. The food belongs to me, and I don't refuse it."

"Look who's giving orders," Antinous said to Eurymachus. "The boy king!" He pushed his footstool in front of him and made like he was picking it up and throwing it. "If everyone would give as I do, we'd soon be rid of your beggar."

Odysseus stood tall in his dirty rags, and talked right back to him in his deep voice. "I see you are a high-ranking nobleman," he said. "You should give a larger crust of bread than all the rest." He opened up his sack, and Antinous made a big show of holding his nose.

"I, too, was once a prince," Master said, "with warriors to command and a lofty house full of servants. I always gave to the homeless. Then Zeus wrecked my fortunes; I was kidnapped by Egyptian pirates. You, too, your fortunes could turn in the beat of a moment. . . ."

"Get away from my table or I'll kick you back to Egypt!"

"Now I see what kind of man you are. A beggar who comes to your own door wouldn't get so much as a grain of salt. Even here, where you're eating another man's food, you begrudge me your scraps."

Red-faced with fury, Antinous was. He grabbed the footstool and sent it crashing against the beggar's back. Master didn't waver; stood there like a rock, he did. The stool hit him just below his shoulder and shattered onto the floor. Telemachus jumped up, boiling with rage.

But Master just turned and went back to his place by the doorway. Stood there and warned them, all eyes on him, too. "Zeus, protector of strangers, has seen this shameful act," he told them. "If there's a god of beggars, Antinous will soon be in his grave, not his marriage bed." He looked at them from underneath his brows, and swept his gaze all around the room. "You men have a choice. Stay joined in this lawless behavior—or leave now. If you stay, you're doomed to heavenly vengeance, and no man here will escape it."

I wanted to stand up and cheer. They all looked so scared, even Eurymachus. "You shouldn't have hit the beggar," he said to Antinous.

"Zeus can pose as a stranger seeking alms," another one said.

A chance to escape Master offered, but not a man got up to leave. They made the bard play the lyre, and turned to dancing. I'm ashamed to say some of our maids were flirting and dancing with them. All this been going on for some time, mind you, but never before out in the open.

The rowdiness was Athena's doing, I'm sure of it. She wanted to make Odysseus fight like a madman when the time came. Master didn't show a thing, just took his seat by the doorway and ate his scraps. Poor soul, he kept looking at the stairs to the women's quarters, where Lady Penelope was. My heart was breaking for how much he was burning to see her.

I went up to my lady's quarters and found her at the loom. "Did you hear what happened to the beggar?" I asked.

She nodded. "Odysseus would be ashamed of such behavior in his own house."

It was on my tongue to tell her, right then and there. Instead, I said, "Don't you want to come down and have a look at the stranger? He's of noble birth, but down on his luck. Maybe he has news that Odysseus is on his way home, even now."

She held up her hand. "No more predictions," she said, smiling sadly. "But I'll go down tonight and hear his story. I can't leave it alone, that someone may have seen him. You, too, Nanny; we're both addicted to the rumors."

I looked at the blue circles under her eyes and wondered if her husband would ever know what courage it took to stay and wait all those years. "Get some rest, then," I said. "You look all done in."

I led her to the couch, and she stretched out like she was grateful for the suggestion. I stayed beside her, the way I used to do with my boys. Sleep came right away. It was a magic sleep—Athena must have sent it—because after a while she woke up glowing with beauty, her skin whiter than ivory, her cheeks flushed.

"I had such a strange dream," she said. "I was taking care of my geese when an eagle came and killed them all. And, Auntie, I have the strangest wish to go downstairs and taunt these men that I've learned to hate with all my heart. . . ."

"Good girl! Go scold them for their plot to get rid of your boy. See what they say, the ruffians. Been off meeting again."

"We should warn Telemachus to stay away from them. But how can he? They're all over the place."

I wanted to tell her his father was home to protect him. How it would have softened her worry.

So lovely she was when she came downstairs that a hush fell over the men, looking at her like they wanted to gobble her up and all her lands, too.

Master never let on. When she smiled a welcome in his direction, he sat there nodding and groveling like he had no words for such a highborn lady. Always such a cool head, that one. His life depended on it, mind you.

She spoke first to Telemachus. "Son, you're not a child anymore. How can you let a stranger be mistreated in our hall? Suppose he were hurt? The shame would be on all of us."

Telemachus answered as best he could. "You're right to scold me," he said to his mother, "but these men outnumber me by a hundred."

That's when Eurymachus sidled over to say there would be hundreds more wooers spilling out of the hall if they could see how beautiful she was.

My lady wasn't fooled by their sweet talk. She pulled her veil around her face and said, "My beauty left me when my husband left for war. All I have now is my son, and I intend to protect him." Then Penelope faced the suitors, standing there like golden Aphrodite, with one arm leaning against a column. "Listen, all of you. Before my husband went to war, he made me promise that when our boy had grown his first beard, I would choose a husband and leave this land."

They all looked at Telemachus, the fools, elbow-ing each other and pointing at the boy's new beard.

"I won't object to my mother's remarriage," Telemachus said after a quick glance at the beggar. "It's the manner of your wooing that's so shameful."

"Those who would court a noble widow bring their own sheep and goats," my lady told them. "They bring their own skins of wine to drink. They compete with one another in bringing fine gifts. And they go home when they're asked to."

"There's truth to what she says," Antinous said, stepping forward. "I propose we make offerings of our love! Let's all send our heralds to bring back gifts. Our lady is obliged to accept them. But"—he lowered his head and turned back to Penelope—"we will none of us go home until you select one of us as your husband."

If Master was surprised by her offer, he never let on. Later, I would make sure he knew she was just luring their gifts, while in her heart she despised each and every one of them. Master would be proud; it was the kind of game he played so well himself.

The queen left then without a backward glance.

"He's not coming home!" Antinous called after her as she climbed the stairs. "He's *dead*! Or else he's chosen *not* to come home, the more fool he!"

Long after she was gone, Odysseus kept his eyes on the doorway to her rooms.

∽ ∽ ∽

Presents arrived all afternoon and into the night, golden earrings and silver bowls, blue-black slaves from Ethiopia. Antinous's herald brought a violet robe with four golden clasps. Eurymachus gave an amber necklace that glowed in the dark. Each gift was displayed to the cheers of the suitors. They kept me running, sending them up to show my lady and then packing them away. By the end of the day, our storerooms were full.

Meanwhile, they kept up their drinking, and the dancing soon turned to fighting. Mark my words, something wicked had entered the hall. Silly quarrels turned to fisticuffs and bloody noses. Black night fell, and still they stayed. I didn't see how we were ever going to get rid of them. I had the maids light torches and pile plenty of wood for kindling.

Odysseus came over to the maid called Melantho. All day he'd been watching her making love eyes at Eurymachus. Everyone knew they were lovers. Shameless hussy, the girl showed not the slightest loyalty to the queen. This after my lady raised her like her own child. A green-eyed, curly-haired imp she was. With no daughter of her own, Mistress gave her pretty clothes and kept her away from all the heavy work.

Master must have been remembering those early days. "Let me keep the torches going," he said to Melantho. "Go upstairs and sit with your lady. Card the wool or spin the yarn. Talk to her, keep her company."

But the minx had no mind to be separated from her worthless boyfriend. "Have you no respect for your betters?" she said. "Go sleep in town, next to the fountain, like the other beggars. The wine must have gone to your head for you to babble on like this."

"Let the beggar stay," Eurymachus shouted. "Stand him next to the torch. The reflection off his bald head can light the hall till morning. . . ."

Master stood his ground, no cringing for the likes of him. "Because you're rich and powerful, you think you can humiliate people like me," he said. "But when Odysseus comes home, these- gates will not open wide enough to let you escape."

"Leave it be, Eurymachus!" one of the suitors yelled.

"My god, we're arguing over a beggar." Another one laughed, nervous like.

Eurymachus picked up a chair and threw it; Master ducked, and it hit a steward. Poor boy, it knocked him over, and wine sloshed all over the floor.

Telemachus had to bang his spear against the wall. *"Fools!"* he called out. "You must be possessed by some god (and this was rightly so!). Look around! You're behaving like lunatics! You've eaten well and drunk your fill. It's time to go home to your beds. Tomorrow is a festival sacred to the archer god Apollo."

Some bit their lips, looking to Antinous. Astonished they were at the boy's words, so like his father he sounded. Gods be praised! My Telemachus went away to Sparta a boy and came back a man! And here he was showing his father he knew how to behave like a king.

"Come now," Telemachus was saying. "Let the cupbearer pour a final libation."

At the boy's signal, heralds went to deliver the wine. Each man poured a libation onto the floor for the deathless gods, took one last swig, and then staggered off to his quarters in town. Eurymachus was too drunk to walk by himself; the hussy Melantho had to support him.

When the last one was gone, a waiting silence settled over the hall. Servants in the corners gave me jittery looks, like they didn't know if they should clean up the mess or run away and hide.

"One last chore," Odysseus said softly. "Nanny, clear the hall. Tell the women to stay in their rooms. We're going to take down the weapons from the walls and lock them in the storeroom. If anyone asks," he said to Telemachus, "tell them you don't want the smoke to ruin them, that Odysseus is on his way home and will be angry to see them covered with soot. No, better yet, tell them it's too easy to start a fight and reach for a weapon. Today we were lucky with a few black eyes. A stabbing would spoil the courting and start a vendetta. Tell them it's for their own protection."

I sent away the servants and ran to fetch the key to the weapons storeroom. When I got back, father and son were removing spears and swords, shields and helmets. These they carried to the storeroom, and a curious light moved above them.

"Did you see that gleam on the rafters?" Telemachus cried out, eyes wide. "Surely the goddess is leading our way."

"Be quiet and accept her gifts," Odysseus whispered. "It's not fitting to ask questions."

After they finished, Odysseus signaled me to reopen the hall. "It's time for you to go to bed" he said, putting his large hand on his son's shoulder. "You've done well, and you need your rest for tomorrow. I'll stay and talk to your mother. Eurycleia, you can bring her down now."

CHAPTER 3

∾

My lady came down right away. You should have seen her! Glowing like a goddess, she was! The maids put her chair next to the fire with her favorite purple throw on top while I brought a chair for the beggar.

Master sat down facing her, hands on his knees, and she fixed on him her wide black eyes with their thick lashes. "I'm sorry you were treated so badly in my house," she said.

"It's not your fault; these men have no shame." He must have been wondering if she still loved him, but his face didn't show a thing. Smooth as milk he was, so good at playing a role.

I brought our finest wine in silver cups. "Sit with us, Nanny, hear his story," Penelope said, always so kind to me, and then, to Odysseus, "Tell us, stranger, who are you and where do you come from?"

He leaned back in his chair and sipped his wine. "My story would only bring you more grief. Surely you have enough of your own."

I was reading her face for signs. Didn't she remember that wonderful deep voice? She did pause a minute, and looked at him strangely.

Yes, it's him! I was screaming inside; I almost gave her a poke in the ribs.

"We would be the last to blame you," she was saying. "The gods have sent us almost twenty years of grief. Eurycleia here nursed my husband, King Odysseus. Took him in her arms right after his birth. It's even worse for me. I've not been allowed to mourn in peace. I'm held hostage by the intruders you saw today—men from as far away as woody Zanthe courting me against my will. I've never given them the slightest encouragement."

He stopped her with an uplifted palm. "Lady Penelope, your loyalty to home and husband will live forever in the memory of men."

Then why can't he trust her? I asked myself. "Tell the stranger about the shroud," I said to Penelope, hoping that would convince him.

"It was a plan to stall them," she said. "I told them that before I chose a husband and left Ithaca, I needed to weave a shroud for my father-in-law, Laertes. His own wife, Odysseus's mother, died years ago. I told them I didn't want to be criticized by the local women if Laertes went to his grave without a fine cloth to cover him." She smiled like a girl, so proud of her scheme. "This went on for three years. I'd weave all day. Then at night, by torchlight, I'd pick out most of the stitches."

"Melantho, she was the one told the suitors," I said, "the girl that went off with Eurymachus."

Penelope sighed. "We don't know for sure, Nanny."

"Wasn't it Eurymachus came and caught you unraveling the stitches?"

"That's when the suitors became truly unmanageable," she said, shaking her head. "I suppose it was Melantho. She's changed so, I can hardly believe it. The point is, I've had to finish the shroud once and for all. I bound it and took it off the loom just last month."

"Beautiful it is, too," I said. "Shows the flotilla of ships to Troy and the great horse."

"I can no longer escape a marriage," Penelope said with another long sigh. "You heard me tell the suitors of my promise. I spoke the truth. When our son grew his first beard, Odysseus wanted me to choose a husband and leave this land I came to as a bride. Would that I could die first. . . ." She lifted her head, remembering her duty as hostess. "Tell us about your travels," she said, leaning forward, and then, the question always in her mind, "Did you ever happen to meet my husband?"

"Aye, My Lady. I knew him on Crete, that's

where I come from. A gale blew him to our shores on his way to Troy. I'm brother to King Idomeneus, Aethon is my name. He'd already gone to war, so I was left to entertain Odysseus and his men."

Color rushed to my lady's cheeks; her dark eyes sparkled. It was always this way when a visitor spoke of him.

"I gave them barley and wine and some sheep. They stayed at our court twelve days before the winds dropped and they went on to Troy."

There she sat, crying over his memory. Master hid his own tears, couldn't give in to the pity in his heart. Such a sad thing, she was mourning for her man, and he was right there in front of her! I glared at him to end her misery.

But then Penelope wouldn't allow herself to trust him, either. There'd been too many liars bringing stories of Odysseus to our court. "I'll give you a test," she said. "Tell me what he was wearing when you first saw him."

"My Lady, that was so long ago." He drank his wine, pretending to think. "All right, let me close my eyes. I'll try to picture him as he was then. Not handsome, but . . . interesting. Broad shoulders, dark blond hair, curly beard."

She smiled through her tears, soaking up every detail.

"He was wearing . . . a woolen cape, red, the color of unmixed wine, and—yes, now I see it—a gold brooch to clasp it, a hunting dog that had just captured a fawn. A remarkable piece—"

"I designed that pin to remind him of his favorite hound!"

"Argos, the old dog in the courtyard today!" I called out. I was caught by his lies in spite of myself—and so was he.

He gave me that same wicked look I knew so well. He said, "All the women were staring at him. His tunic was of lustrous fabric, smooth as the outer skin of an onion. Of course I don't know if these garments came from home or were given to him after he left. People were always giving him things. He was an extraordinary man."

She clasped her hands together. "*I* gave him that cape, and the tunic, too! I wove the cloth myself. On the day he left, I fastened on the brooch."

He was quiet, fingering his goblet, and then said, softly, "Telemachus has his first beard."

"I know. I'm ready to give in to their demands. Telemachus is grown, he doesn't need me anymore. And day after day, he sees them eating up his livelihood. Even worse, the villains are plotting to kill him. If I marry one of them, the rest will go away and leave him alone." She was silent a moment, biting her lip, then, "Listen, Nanny, here's my plan. Tomorrow I'm going to bring down my husband's great bow. The man who can string it and shoot an arrow through a line of axes, he's the one I'll marry."

"Odysseus used to do that trick," I said. "All the handles in a row, and he'd shoot right through them. All twelve axes! He'd stand a long way off, too."

"What about today's gifts?" he asked. "Wasn't there one that pleased you above all others?"

"I only proposed the gifts to gather riches for my son. They've drained our treasury with their endless banquet. It's only fair they should pay something back."

"Good," he said. "Tomorrow's the feast of Apollo, the archer, a fitting day for a shooting contest."

When I left to check on the maids, the two were talking like old friends. Penelope was describing her dream, about the geese and the eagle that came and killed them.

Servants were scouring cups and bowls, sponging down tables, sweeping the floor. I wanted it done right before I let them go off to their beds. Didn't want to face a mess in the morning.

Later we banked the torches. The queen and the beggar were bent toward each other in the glow of the fire. He was analyzing her dream.

"Clearly," he said, "Odysseus is the eagle, and the geese are the suitors. He's coming to kill them all. . . ."

"I know you're trying to be kind, but I've stopped believing in miracles."

"Lady, it's not just your dream. I heard it from

Dulichion merchants. Odysseus has made it as far as the mainland! He's collecting gifts from the Greek heroes. He didn't want to come back empty-handed."

"If only this were true, I would shower you with gifts." She shrugged and looked away. "But Odysseus is never coming home. I have to accept that."

"You have my oath, My Lady. He's very near."

I came and stood behind her, my hands on the back of her chair. "Tell her!" I said to him, just mouthing the words.

"Besides," she was saying, "your interpretation doesn't make sense. In the dream I wept to see my geese killed. Yet I loathe the suitors and would rejoice to see them dead."

"Here's my explanation. There's one thing about the suitors you can perhaps appreciate. Think about it." He paused, choosing his words. "Wasn't there a time—maybe just an instant—when you blamed your husband for going off and leaving you?"

She didn't answer. She sat there tracing the whorls of silver on the arm of her chair.

"Didn't you ever wonder about other women?" he asked after a silence. "Not that any woman could rival you. You have my oath on that, too!"

I glared down at him, but he refused to meet my eyes. What kind of test was this? What was he doing teasing her with other women? "Men, I'll never understand their mysterious ways. Worse than the gods, they are," I said, and turned away.

I heard her take a breath and let it out slowly. "Yes, maybe Antinous is right. Maybe Odysseus is off somewhere and chooses not to come home."

"That's not true!" he interrupted.

But she stopped him with a raised palm. "What has all that got to do with my geese?" she said.

He smiled, shaking his head. "Just that part of you might be flattered that so many fine lords are fighting to be your husband. Still, none will escape their doom, just like the geese!"

"Stranger, I don't agree with your reasoning, but you've managed to entertain me far into the night. I could stay here listening to your stories, except that we all need our sleep for tomorrow. Besides, Nanny is making eye signals for us to close down the hall."

She got up from her chair. "Eurycleia, fix him a bed and pile it with our best comforters. Good night, brother of Idomeneus. Tomorrow we'll get you a bath and fine clothes. You can sit beside Telemachus and watch the contest with the bow."

Odysseus refused the couch and stretched out on a pile of sheepskins on the floor of the vestibule. I came and tucked a warm cloak over him.

"She deserves to know," I whispered.

"It's safer this way." He rolled over on his side.

"She's done nothing to make you doubt her virtue. Thundering Zeus, you have *my* oath on that!"

"Go to sleep, Nanny, you're bossier than ever."

But I didn't sleep. Just like when he was a child, I sat in the corner and listened for him to lie still and breathe deeply. Such a restless soul, so full of plans, he always fought the gift of sleep.

We heard two more maids running off to the suitors' beds, giggling as they crossed the courtyard. Odysseus beat his breast and muttered in frustration. Must have wanted to jump up and strangle them right there.

Then, gods be praised, I heard Athena come to him, heard her silver voice in the shadows. Scolded him, Bright Eyes did. Told him to trust her and give up his suffering and scheming. She must have covered him with sweet sleep, because suddenly all was quiet.

I stayed in my chair. I didn't want to leave my master. This was the best day of my life. I'd waited nineteen years; I wasn't going to miss a minute of it. I must have dozed, though. Toward dawn I heard Penelope call out in her dreams, "Odysseus, don't leave me!"

And he stirred in his sleep and murmured her name.

CHAPTER 4

∞

I slept until after dawn, more's the shame. Master was up and gone, his cloak folded on a bench. Right away, I gave the serving women their orders and sent four maids to fetch water from the spring. Told them not to dawdle. Then my boy Telemachus was down looking for his father, his two hounds jumping at his feet.

Feeling his oats, the boy was. "Why did my mother let our visitor sleep on the floor?" he asked me. "I thought I could count on her to behave sensibly."

"We'll have none of your disrespect, because none is due," I said, clucking my tongue. "Good thing your daddy is back to keep you in line."

Rascal dodged when I tried to box his ears. I said, "Your mother offered bed and bath, clean clothes, too, right proper, Master wouldn't have it. You ever argue with him when he has his mind set? Went to sleep on the porch, and I covered him with a cloak. Off with you, ask him yourself. I've no time for dilly-dallying with foolish questions."

The swineherd Eumaeus came after that, driving four hogs for the day's feast. We weren't ready, but the uninvited guests came trooping back as always with their empty bellies. Somewhere in all the hustle bustle, Master took Eumaeus outside, and Mentor, too. Told them who he was, showed them the scar. Both were weeping with joy, but Master was all business. Told Eumaeus it was his job to bring the bow to him after all the suitors had their chance to string it. Then Mentor was to go outside and double-bolt the gates. None of the dolts noticed anything, mind you. Too busy butchering pigs, filling their wine bowls, spreading fleece on the benches to make themselves comfortable. After that, they were too busy feeding their faces.

Telemachus put the master at a small table and told the suitors to leave him alone. "This is my father's house, and mine by birthright," he said. "Today you'll control yourselves or I'll have you thrown out."

Most looked surprised the boy would talk like that. Only Antinous had a comeback. "Fighting words from our boy king. We're obliged to obey," he said, rolling his eyes, and then, under his breath, "until we can shut his mouth for good."

They all snickered.

"We'll see that your beggar gets his fair share!"
Eurymachus yelled. He picked up an ox hoof and
heaved it at Odysseus. Master ducked, and it landed
against the wall. Always throwing things, the louts
were.

"Good thing it didn't hit him," Telemachus said
between his teeth, "because I would have sent my
spear through your throat."

Dead silence. Who knows what kind of riot
would have broken out, but Penelope was coming
down the stairs with two of her ladies, and in her
arms was Odysseus's great Scythian bow. The frame
was longer than most men's arm span, made of hick-
ory with a casing of ox hide on the outer rim.

"I have a contest to propose, in the name of
Apollo the archer," she said to them. "The first man
who can string my husband's bow and shoot it
through twelve ax handles will be my chosen husband."

What an uproar, all of them pointing at the bow
and yelling how big it was. "I'll marry him and go
away from this house, which I'll remember forever in
my dreams," my lady was saying, but her voice was
swallowed by the oafs shouting challenges at each
other.

Telemachus was already out in the courtyard
with Mentor helping him, that quick the boy was to
get started. He threw off his purple cloak and dug a
trench, lined the axes in a row. His father must have

explained everything, and the boy did it just right; the axes straight as a plumb line with the round handles on top and the blades buried tight in the ground. After that, Telemachus marched over and took the bow from his mother's hands. Couldn't resist a try himself. Twice the boy bent it; third time he almost had it. Would have strung it, too, but Master made a signal with his eyebrows, and Telemachus smiled and put it down.

Fools all laughed like that was the funniest thing they ever saw. Then Antinous said they should come have a try in the order they were sitting, starting with the man closest to the wine bowl. That was Leodes. His nickname was Wineface, which gives you a good idea of his skill as an archer. Hands so soft and uncalloused, he couldn't bend the bow at all. The fools laughed some more, but that laughter would turn to screams before the hour was over.

Antinous sent for some lard from the pantry, and they oiled the wood so it would be more supple. A whole string of men tried and failed before Eurymachus picked it up. He managed to bend it, but not enough. Mumbling and sweating all over his tunic, he went and warmed it over the fire and tried again two more times, but it wouldn't budge any further.

"Don't give up so soon," Antinous told him. "Isn't this day sacred to Apollo? We'll send for more sheep and make a sacrifice to him. Leave the axes planted in the court. We can try again this evening."

Filthy liar probably decided he couldn't do it and was looking to find some way out. The suitors were quick to agree, though, and the stewards mixed another go-around of wine. That's when Odysseus stood up.

"Gentlemen! Later you'll have another chance; the archer god will favor the best among you. For now I ask you to let me have a try with the bow. I want to see if my hands are as strong as they once were."

The men's eyes darted to Antinous. He turned slowly to face the beggar, hands on his hips. "The nerve of you! It's not enough that you sit and eat in this fine company? You actually think you have rights?"

"This man is Telemachus's guest!" Penelope called out. "Let him try his strength. He's not a contender! He has no intention of marrying me."

"We never thought he was," Eurymachus said, and he laughed nervous like. "Still, imagine the dishonor if we can't string the bow and a beggar manages to do it."

"That shame would be trivial compared to what you've already earned." Penelope's mouth was smiling, but anger flashed in her eyes.

"Talk of honor or dishonor is pointless with these men," Telemachus interrupted. "Mother, I ask you to take your women upstairs. Go work at your looms, and let me settle things here. The bow is mine. . . . If I wish to give it to my guest, I will."

Penelope must have been proud to see Telemachus acting like a prince and taking command. Now that I look back, I think the boy was also protecting her from some sights that no mother should have to see. While the women were climbing the stairs, Eumaeus went and picked up the bow from the table, and Telemachus pointed his chin at the beggar. Right away the fools yelled like they were wounded.

"Look at the swineherd! Is he crazy?"

"What are you doing, Pigman?"

"Drop it or we'll feed you to your dogs!"

Eumaeus dropped the bow, that's how frightened the poor man was.

"Uncle, I gave you an order!" Telemachus called out.

Eumaeus picked up the bow again. Head down, he plowed straight away through the crowd, put it in Master's hands, and bent to hear his words. Then he came over to me, eyes round in his face. The louts were complaining and arguing so loud, he had to shout.

"My good nurse, Master says you should . . . uh, what was that? I'm all befuddled. Take the serving women and lock them in their quarters. Stay outside the door." Poor soul, he had to stop, eyes squeezed shut, to remember the rest. "And . . . don't come down till we call you. No matter what you hear."

I rounded up the servants and herded them out

the great doors. I had to give a pinch to that hussy
Melantho. She knew something was up, mind you.
While I was at this, I saw Mentor run outside. His job
was to double-bolt the doors and slip back into the
hall through the pantry.

I got them all locked in the servants' quarters.
Melantho was scared, she and three others who had
boyfriends down there. Pleaded with me to let them out,
but I slammed the door and locked it from the outside.
They were banging on it and crying my name when I
turned away and went back downstairs. I wanted one
look at Master taking his hall back. Just one.

When I came into the courtyard through the
pantry, Mentor was already on guard. He started to
push me back inside, but before I could argue with
him, both of us had to stop and stare.

His hands full of love, like a bard with his harp,
my master was fingering his bow.

"Maybe he has one just like it back home," one
of the oafs said, laughing.

Without any grunting or straining, Master bent
the ends together and looped the string onto the
groove at the tip of the wood frame. He slid his hand
down the cord and gave it a *ping* to make sure it was
sound after all those years. Still sitting on his stool,
Master was. Didn't even need to stand up. He reached
for an arrow, and set it in the bow. Then he took aim
and sent it zinging through all twelve handles!

The suitors jostled one another and craned their

necks to see. Right then Zeus sent a clap of thunder, and all got quiet, their faces blanched white.

Odysseus sprang up onto the great stone threshold, in front of the locked doors. Telemachus buckled on his sword, grabbed his spear, and raced over to his father. My heart swelled in my chest to see the two of them united in battle. Mentor and me, we were crying tears of joy.

I had to drag myself away. I wanted to see Antinous get the first arrow, but Master likes his orders obeyed. I went up to the women's quarters, where the queen's maids were huddled in a corner, clutching one another, not saying a word. Penelope was stretched out on her couch in the deepest sleep short of death. Sent by the goddess, it was, because she never even stirred through all the screaming and slamming.

Antinous was first to die, Zeus be thanked. I have the story from Eumaeus. Just reaching for his wine, the villain was, still cracking jokes about the beggar, making himself believe the trick with the axes was some kind of accident. Odysseus shot him right through his lying throat. Arrow came out the other side. Blood spurting from his mouth, he fell forward and knocked over a table, bread and meat, wine and blood all over the floor.

Some of the idiots still didn't realize what was happening, even when they saw their leader's blood mixing with the wine. They jumped up, yelling and shaking their fists at Odysseus.

"You'll die for this!"

"We'll tear your eyes out!"

"Think you can shoot arrows into men?"

Poor fools. Then they looked up at the walls, where spears and shields used to hang. Athena gave Master back his glowing health, his thick, curly hair, and his muscular legs. And still some of the younger ones didn't know who he was.

"Worthless parasites!" Master yelled. "You never thought I'd return from Troy to punish you!"

They spun around and were terrified to see all the doors locked.

Eurymachus kept his wits, I have to give the man credit for that. He stepped forward and pointed to Antinous's body. "Here's the ringleader," he said to Odysseus. "He's the one who led us in this madness. He was plotting to kill your son so his own heirs would inherit. He's got his reward. But, please, spare your own people. We'll pay back all we ate and drank. Twenty oxen each man. You know my father will pay a king's ransom—"

Master smiled a smile that would chill a man to his bones. "No, Eurymachus. Not for all your father's wealth."

Saw how it was then, Eurymachus did. "Take out your swords!" he shouted. "Let's charge in a cohort! You lads over there, throw down the tables to use as shields!"

Odysseus's arrow ripped through his liver, and

Eurymachus fell to the floor, howling. One by one, Master picked off a dozen more. Held them off with his arrows while Telemachus ran to get him a sword and shield. Still, they kept coming. Formed a line and rushed him, all trying to reach the pantry door. Telemachus stabbed one in the back who was coming right at his father with a spear. Ran him through, the boy did.

Athena was down there the whole time. Eumaeus says she took the form of old Mentor; others think she flew up to the rafters and directed the battle from above. Upstairs in the women's quarters we heard the groans and screams, the smash of tables and *thuds* of bodies. We heard it when they stampeded for the front gates, the poor fools beating their fists against massive doors that were latched from the outside with ship's cable. Toward the end, we heard some of them calling for their mothers.

Phoenius, the bard, pleaded for his life at Odysseus's knees, right next to Zeus's altar. Still holding on to his lyre, he was. "Spare me, great king. Telemachus will tell you, they forced me to come and sing for them."

"Yes, this one is blameless," Telemachus said, running up. "And the herald Medon, too. He always took good care of me when I was little. . . ."

Medon heard the boy in all the ruckus, that's the wonder. "Here I am, Master!" a voice called out. Medon climbed out from under a table, and they all had a good laugh.

That's when Master sent for me. I found him standing in a pile of corpses, spattered with blood like a lion that's just eaten its kill.

I threw back my head to shout the alleluia of victory, but Odysseus stopped me. "It's not fitting to glory in their deaths," he said. "The gods have sent their revenge. It's over. Nanny, how many of our maids have been disloyal?"

"Fifty women, you have, trained by me and my lady. Do their duties well, My Lord. Only four been traipsing off after the suitors."

"Bring them down. We'll see they're hanged in the outer court.

"Good riddance!" I spat on the ground. "Hussies earned that and more for sleeping with the enemy."

"The servants can pile the bodies in the yard next to the wall," he said. "Have them scrub down the tables and chairs, scrape the floor with spades. We'll sprinkle it with sulfur afterward and fumigate the hall." And then, pointing at Telemachus, he said, "Your mother's not to see any of this."

I didn't go for Penelope until after we finished the cleanup. Still lost in that magical sleep, she was.

"My Lady! Wake up, he's home!" I was shaking her and chuckling at the same time. "Odysseus is back! He's killed all the intruders. Blood and entrails all over the place!" I remembered Master's instructions and added, "All cleaned up now, Mistress. They're all gone! Come see."

Her eyes opened with such a look of pain.

"Your son was fighting right alongside his father. You'll be so proud to see them together!"

"How dare you wake me with such lies, and this the best sleep I've had since my husband left home."

"It's true! He's downstairs waiting for you, the old beggar the louts were abusing, but that was just a disguise. Telemachus knew all along. Been keeping his mouth shut. And I saw Master's scar—the one the boar gave him. You can take my life if it's not true."

She sat up in bed, clutching the sheet between her breasts. "If all the suitors are dead, then it's clearly some god's doing. One of the immortals has punished them for their evil deeds. How could Odysseus engage them single-handed?"

"Always so wary! True enough, Master had help from Athena. Bright Eyes it was sent you that precious sleep. She's been watching over you, too. She's given him back all his beauty. Come downstairs and see." And when she didn't answer, I said, "Don't you want to congratulate your son?"

"Yes, Telemachus," she said slowly, and still she sat there holding on to the sheet. "And if all the suitors are really dead, I want to thank whoever killed them for me."

CHAPTER 5

∾

S he's down here in the hall with him now. Took the chair nearest the door, and he's leaning against a column. It's been a standoff ever since we got here, like the two of them posing for a wall painting.

Why won't she look at him? Is she afraid to let herself believe this is the real husband after all those impostors? Or maybe she thinks he's one of the gods taking human form. Plenty of that going on, too, and comes to no good for the poor mortal woman who gets bedded and pregnant. Always such a cautious thing, my lady was, ever since she came here as a bride.

Then, too, she's almost as crafty as Master. Could be she's making him suffer. Could be she's mad nobody told her about the beggar. Now she's looking over at him like she's imagining all the other women.

All right, so there were women along the way. Zeus Almighty, she ought to let that drop. Came home to her, didn't he? Cleared her house of vermin. Poor man, covered with blood, all sweaty and dirty. Must think she doesn't want him back. Must be driving him crazy. It's driving me crazy.

Telemachus can't stand it any longer. "What a heartless woman you are!" he says to his mother. "Your husband returns from twenty years of hardship, and you won't say a word?"

Gods be praised! She's lifting her head. She's going to say something.

"If this is your father, we'll know one another in our own time." She looks only at Telemachus. "We'll have our own signs, our own secret ways of knowing."

Odysseus breaks into a smile, relieved like. "Don't scold your mother. How could she know me like this, spattered in blood? I'll go bathe and dress," he says to her.

She doesn't answer.

That gets three of us moving, anyway. Odysseus tells Telemachus to go arrange proper funeral rites for the corpses in the yard, that Athena will make it right with the families, so there will be no revenge. I go get a clean tunic and a purple cape for my master while the serving women bathe him and rub his body with oil. Radiant like a god he is when he steps out of the bath. Athena's covered him with beauty.

He sits down facing his wife; looks her right in the eye. And still she can't believe—or won't believe. She's staring down at her hands, not saying a word. All her troubles are over. Why can't she just accept her good fortune? I want to take her by the shoulders and shake her.

We hear servants' voices outside. Somewhere in the courtyard, a bird chirps. I'm wishing Telemachus would come back and do something. Finally, Master jumps to his feet. Fed up with waiting, he is. "What other woman would have such a heart of stone?" he says, and then, "Nanny, make up my bed. I'll sleep alone."

Penelope signals me then. She says, "Better yet, have the servants take our bed from the bridal chamber and bring it out here for him."

Oh, she's a sly one. I look from one to the other, trying to figure out what game she's playing now.

"After all," she's saying, "he built the bed himself, he should enjoy it."

Maybe she wants to punish him for leaving her alone so long. Or she's still got her mind on those other women.

Speechless, he is. Glaring at her from under his eyebrows.

"Cover it with blankets to keep him warm," she adds.

"My bed!" he bellows. "You cut our bed from its roots in the earth? Zeus Thunderer, woman, you've gone too far!"

He's beet red and sputtering, standing over her chair like he wants to strangle her. "Who dared move my bed? Have those no-good suitors dug it out of the earth? By god, they'd have to dismantle the whole room!" he shouts at me. "I laid it out around that olive tree, made the trunk into one of the bedposts."

That does it for her. She jumps out of the chair and falls into his arms. Her legs don't look like they can support her. Good thing, because now he has to grab hold of her.

"Don't yell at me, Odysseus," she says. "I've hardened myself against the frauds and the lies. I had to be sure, and that was the proof I needed. No other man has seen the bed. It's still rooted in the earth; over by the window the branches touch the ceiling now. And only the real Odysseus would have reacted with such outrage." She smiles, then, thinking about it. "If you had been a god, you would have behaved with more restraint."

She takes his face in her hands. "I wanted to know if you could still act from your heart. That you're not always going to be calculating your next move."

"Did I pass that test, too?"

She strokes his cheek and kisses his lips for an answer.

Tears well in his eyes, and suddenly he lets down the weight of his longing and weeps in her arms. Gods be praised, at last he can believe he's standing there holding his dear, faithful wife. That she wants him as much as he wants her.

"There's never been another man," she tells him between kisses. "I would have waited forever."

"What about the contest with the bow?"

"I knew none of them would be able to string it. I was buying time."

"And you have my oath, the one I swore last night. No other woman could rival you."

I'm thinking he should keep his mouth shut about the women, but she doesn't take offense. He pulls away and looks at her, still so lovely. He says, "I'm talking about your guile as well as your beauty."

They're crying and laughing together. He's kissing her eyes, her cheeks, her forehead.

I stand there shaking my head, my own tears flowing. What happiness to see them teasing each other with words the way they used to. Thundering Zeus, he thought he was testing her, and she was getting ready to test him! The only time in all these years anyone outfoxed him—and it was his own wife did it!

Two like minds, they are. I always said that to anyone who would listen. Penelope is his equal in strategies. No wonder there was such harmony between them.

Hand in hand, they go off to their olive tree bed. I made it up for them already. Sprinkled lavender under the sheets to give them a fragrance and tucked in a fertility charm just for luck. My lady may well have some childbearing years left. With help from the goddess, they could still give me another heir to raise.

Long into the night I hear them talking softly whenever I pass by the door. He's spinning his adventures for her. The whole world he can give her now, but he's different from that restless boy who fought the gift of sleep. He'll not go wandering, not for all the gold and glory on this earth. He'll hold on to his Penelope like a shipwrecked sailor hugs the shore.

Still, I wager my lady won't be taking any chances. I picture her lying there with her white arms around his neck, and I have to smile. She's listening and marveling at his stories, all the while telling herself that's the end of that. Raider of cities, master of disguises, that's the stuff of legends now. Till death comes to claim him—and I pray that's a long way off—she'll hold on to her man and never again let him go voyaging.

AUTHOR'S EPILOGUE

∾

As a child hooked on the myths, I was both fascinated and frustrated by *The Odyssey*, especially when the women characters left their endless weaving to make brief, intriguing appearances in the men's hall. I always wanted to know how they felt about what was going on. Did Helen enjoy having the world's most beautiful face? Did Penelope blame her for the great war? And why did Circe keep changing men into pigs? So many stories left untold.

I suppose I'm retelling these myths to answer my own questions. The story of how Penelope and Odysseus came to be married was never told in the original epic, composed by a Greek poet named Homer in the eighth century B.C. Homer is also believed to have composed an earlier poem, *The Iliad*, about the Trojan War.

But long before these two epics were ever written down, ancient people used to sit around and tell stories of this war, stories probably stemming from a real Trojan War centuries before. The Romans retold these stories, too, changing Odysseus's name to Ulysses and giving their own names to the Greek gods and godesses. Odysseus and Penelope were as familiar to the ancients as our media heroes are to us. So Homer didn't need to start at the beginning. He jumped into the middle of the story with Odysseus held captive on Kalypso's island.

I wanted to start with the first meeting of Penelope and Odysseus. According to custom, Penelope's husband would have been chosen by her father. I like to think she chose him herself, that she saw this broad-shouldered, cocky warrior and made up her mind to have him, that love struck like sweet poison coursing through her veins. Such gutsy devotion to her man would better explain Penelope's famous loyalty in Homer's *Odyssey*, where she manages a kingdom without a husband for almost twenty years, all the while refusing a host of lusty young warriors.

This wasn't a one-sided passion; Odysseus was devoted to Penelope as well. To get home to her, he leaves the blissful luxury of Circe's palace and risks Poseidon's rage in the open sea. At his next landfall he ignores Kalypso when she tells him that his wife will grow old and wrinkled. (In fact, thirty-eight, my estimate of Penelope's age, *was* considered old in those days.) Later, Odysseus turns down another marriage offer from the exquisite Nausicaa.

ODYSSEUS'S MYTHICAL JOURNEY

Some scholars see all three temptresses—Circe, Kalypso, and Nausicaa—as necessary trials in Odysseus's quest for his own true destiny. According to this view, recently popularized in the writings of Joseph Campbell, our hero undertakes a mythical adventure called the hero's journey. Like other Polynesian, Norse, and African heroes, Odysseus leaves the real world of Troy's battlefields and is blown off course into a dreamscape of monsters and witches. He makes mighty enemies, like the sea god Poseidon. Even the ordinary people he meets have supernatural powers. The Lotus-eaters have magic fruit that erases all memory; the Phaiakians have magic ships that skim across the water as fast as a thought.

Odysseus needs to outsmart the monsters in order to survive. When he meets Circe, Kalypso, and Nausicaa, he must withstand the temptation to abandon his wife and son. And with each challenge, he becomes a better man. Gradually, he even learns to master the pride that had caused him to reveal his real name to the Cyclops Polyphemus, and for which foolishness Circe makes fun of him in my retelling. The mythical hero isn't perfect. He usually has a personality flaw—often his pride—and the journey to overcome this inner demon parallels his outer adventures.

A turning point in both journeys for Odysseus occurs when Kalypso offers him immortality. If he were to accept her offer, he would not only live like a god, he would become one. In my story, Odysseus's refusal was what finally convinced Athena to intercede on his behalf.

MYTHOLOGICAL TYPECASTING

From Homer's Mentor up through Obi-Wan Kenobi in *Star Wars*, the wise guide has been a familiar figure. What's unusual about *The Odyssey* is that this central character is female, the goddess Athena. Although Circe overcomes her dark nature to assist Odysseus for a time, it's Athena who's his real protector. Sometimes she's disguised as old Mentor, but the real mentoring action in *The Odyssey* comes from her.

Another mythical character is the trickster. *The Odyssey* is full of schemes and identity shifting. Penelope tricks the suitors with her loom, and her husband with their bed. Circe changes men into pigs, lions, and wolves. Athena disguises her own appearance and doctors up Odysseus so that he can appear more or less attractive as needed.

Odysseus himself, Homer's "man of twists and turns," is ideally suited for survival. He is tough, ingenious, calculating. And beyond this everyday resourcefulness, he must finally be willing to descend into hell and experience a kind of rebirth. Odysseus accomplishes this twice: First, he visits the prophet Teresias in Hades and lives to tell about it. Later, on the Phaiakian ship bearing him home, he falls into a deathlike sleep. After this second rebirth, he leaves the magical world and accepts the simple life of home and family.

He comes back to this real world more responsible

for others, not just devoted to his own fame. Like Dorothy in *The Wizard of Oz*, like the prodigal son in the Bible, Odysseus has learned that there's no place like home.

But this isn't the only way of interpreting our ancient story. In the world of myths, we can always shift perspective, and it's not difficult, after all, to see Penelope as the hero.

THE HEROINE'S JOURNEY

In my story I wanted to remind readers of the quiet heroism of Penelope's life journey, for she, too, has much to teach us. She watches her husband sail away, furious that she can do nothing to stop him. He's left all things in her hands, and for twenty years, she lives unloved and unprotected. As estate manager, she's expected to supervise servants, worry about dwindling food reserves, discipline her adolescent son, and always live up to her reputation as a model of composure. In *The Odyssey*, she's eternally self-possessed, sensible, but there must have been times she wanted to scream and throw things. Every morning when she came downstairs, there was her hall packed with a hundred brawling, carousing young louts who would leave spilled wine, dirty dishes, and greasy tables to be wiped down when they finally staggered off to bed. Never in all those years did she take a lover; they were none of them any match for her. And always she lived with a crushing uncertainty, not knowing if her husband was dead or somewhere else with some other woman, choosing not to return.

In one scene I have Eurycleia watching her mistress sleep, wondering if Odysseus would ever know what courage it has taken his wife to wait all those years. But our heroine does more than weep and wait. I think the story's central moral dilemma belongs to her. Just as Odysseus must choose between magical luxury and his wife and child, Penelope must choose between husband and son. If she gives in to the suitors' ultimatum and marries one of them, the others will go away, and so will the death threats against Telemachus. What a terrible choice: Leave home in order to protect her son's life and fortune, or stay and remain true to her husband's memory? She manages to postpone the inevitable once again by proposing the contest with the bow, which gives Odysseus the perfect opportunity to kill off his rivals.

Finally, there's the famous bed test to illustrate

Penelope's resourcefulness. When she refuses to acknowledge her husband and tells the nurse to have the marriage bed moved to the courtyard, she's probably (understandably) getting even for twenty years of wandering, and for all the women along the way. Most readers have already guessed that Penelope knows who this man is. And she knows he knows the secret of their olive tree bed. But when she proposes moving it, the great man becomes unglued, the only time in all his adventures that he acts without calculations. He looks like he wants to strangle her. "Did one of those no-good suitors dig it out of the ground?" he bellows. (Translation: "Has one of those no-good suitors been in my bed?")

I think this unrestrained yelling is precisely what Penelope wanted to hear. Odysseus's iron self-control has kept him alive all these years, but Penelope needs to know if her husband can still act "from the heart." Eurycleia, watching this final drama, understands both levels of the test. The old nurse says with a chuckle, ". . . he thought he was testing her, and she was getting ready to test him! The only time in all these years anyone outfoxed him. And it was his own wife did it!"

JOURNEY'S END

Some later sources paint a darker ending for the reunited spouses. One Arcadian tale has Odysseus banish Penelope when he learns she's been unfaithful after all. She gives birth to the unruly goat god Pan as a result of passionate orgies with the suitors. An even more curious tradition has Odysseus murdered (accidentally) by Telegonus, a son he fathered with Circe. For reasons difficult for modern readers to fathom, Penelope takes Odysseus's body back to Circe's island for burial. There she marries Telegonus, and her son Telemachus marries Circe!

I prefer Homer's happy ending, with Odysseus and Penelope together in their olive tree bed, and Athena holding back the dawn to give them time to catch up on almost twenty years. Penelope tells of her struggle with the suitors. Odysseus tells the story of his travels, which ends with a forecast of his own death. According to the prophet Teresias's predictions, Odysseus must walk inland carrying an oar from his ship until he's so far from the sea that the people don't know what an oar is. There he must plant the oar and burn offerings to Poseidon. If he accomplishes this task, the gods will send a gentle death at the end of a long and peaceful life, one that Odysseus now knows how to value.

IS THE MYTH REAL?

Scholars are divided over whether we can trace Odysseus's travels to actual places in the Aegean and western Mediterranean, where, by Homer's day, Greek civilization had begun to spread. Still, some of us enjoy speculating about a real hero on a real journey. Geographical clues in *The Odyssey* would locate the Lotus-eaters somewhere on the coast of North Africa. In Sicily, an island at the toe of Italy's boot, locals will show you the actual rocks the Cyclops Polyphemus threw down at Odysseus. Some scholars have suggested Scandinavia as the home of the savage Laestragonians. Gozo, a Mediterranean island near Malta, claims the nymph Kalypso's enchanted cave, and tour guides on the Greek island of Corfu can take you to the bay where Odysseus appeared to Nausicaa with only a branch to hide his nakedness. Ithaca is still the name of an island off the eastern Coast of Greece; its Vathy Harbor fits the description of the bay between two headlands where Odysseus was finally put ashore. So far there are few archaeological findings to support claims for *The Odyssey* sites, but similar clues from *The Iliad* have led archaeologists to excavate the ruins of Troy near the Dardanelles in modern-day Turkey.

Whether or not Odysseus and Penelope actually walked the earth, their story lives on today in movies and miniseries and in our language. A mentor (from the Greek word for "mind" or "power") is a wise old guide; an odyssey a long, adventurous voyage. Lotus-eaters live in drug-induced bliss. A Penelope's Web is a project that never gets finished. A Penelope is a faithful wife, while sirens are dangerously fascinating women. Odysseus designed the Trojan Horse to get his concealed warriors inside the great walls of Troy, where they launched their fatal attack. At the end of the twentieth century, a Trojan Horse is a computer virus introduced into a system disguised as a virus cleaner.

The myths survive because, beyond entertaining us, they help us understand ourselves and our families—our own monsters and witches—and our own mortality. After three thousand years we still identify with Penelope's devotion, with Nausicaa's desperate eagerness to become a woman. We still encounter obstacles and suffer conflicting loyalties. We're fooled by tricksters and hope to find ourselves a mentor to sort it all out. And love can still strike like sweet poison, coursing through our veins. Just as a classic heroine is learning from her adventures, grappling with her flaws and wanting to become a better human being, so are we. And just as Odysseus comes contentedly home—to himself—we, too, must find ourselves at the end of our journey. But the poet T. S. Eliot says this best, so I'll end the book with his words.

> We shall not cease from exploration,
> and at the end of all our exploring
> we shall arrive where we started
> and know the place for the first time.

CLEMENCE MCLAREN
retells more tales in

INSIDE THE WALLS OF TROY:

"These ancient stories are made as fresh and vivid as any modern tale by the electrifying characters and sensual details. By the time the tragedy has unfolded, readers will no longer think of Helen, Penelope, Achilles, and Odysseus as dull entries in a history text but will recognize them as gripping, fascinating personalities."—*Booklist*

APHRODITE'S BLESSING:

"Expertly retold . . . McLaren endows her classical protagonists with new dimensions, making them vulnerable yet courageous, compassionate yet steel-willed. She artfully preserves the ambience of myth while offering an insightful glimpse of women struggling in a male-dominated world."

—*Publishers Weekly*

Available from Atheneum Books for Young Readers

DISCOVER
CYNTHIA VOIGT'S
EPIC KINGDOM SEQUENCE

JACKAROO: "Intense and elegantly written."
— *School Library Journal*

"A rich story within a story that one is loath to desert, only to discover that the original plot is equally intriguing.... A wonderfully exciting tale."
— *San Francisco Chronicle*

"Swift, many-layered, tense."
— *Publishers Weekly*

ELSKE: An ALA Best Book for Young Adults

"A richly dense, compelling tale. The writing is at some times breathtaking.... Characterization is richly detailed."
— *School Library Journal*

"For readers who enjoy probing the studies of ties that bind, this will illuminate some hidden corners of the human spirit."— *Kirkus*